Ignite

Dedication: This book is dedicated to our own angel baby, Carson. You've always been my inspiration to never take a day for granted and to never give up, ever.

Love Mommy

Copyright © 2015 By: Holly Mortimer
All Rights Reserved
Published By: Holly Mortimer
Digital Edition
ISBN 978-1517094577
All Rights Reserved

Sign up to receive exclusive content and exciting news:
www.hollymortimer.com

Email me at:
info@hollymortimer.com

Find me on Facebook:
https://www.facebook.com/hollymortimerromancewriter

.Tweet to me at:
https://twitter.com/Mortimerwrites

Check out my Goodreads Page:
https://www.goodreads.com/author/show/13494676.Holly_Mortimer

Chapter 1

Frankie

My pulse was soaring and I was fighting for a clear, deep breath. He was here and he was drunk and looking to take his anger out on me. I had to hide. I had to keep quiet. This laboured breathing wasn't helping. I silently berated myself for coming back to get my things. I knew it was risky, but I gave myself a break. The timing would never be perfect.

I hugged my knees to my chest as best I could in this condition, and waited. I wished I had the super power to see through things and to hear things coming miles away. I was a bundle of nerves just waiting to unravel. Thankfully, the closet was spacious and I had tucked myself into a corner, but it seemed useless. He knew I was in the house, it was just a matter of time before he had searched every available hiding spot and found me. My only chance at making it out was to be patient, find an opening and make a run for it.

I muted my phone so the 911 operator who was currently trying to get me to talk to her wouldn't give my location away. I hoped that she heard me when I whispered my address into the phone. I couldn't risk giving away my location to him before I was ready. I still wanted to keep the connection open so that when and if I could manage it, I would unmute her and she could hear the violence I was enduring. If nothing else, I could perhaps finally get some third party evidence as to what was happening.

I quieted my breath and forced myself to become still. And then I felt it. The change in the air when another presence is close. A shadow flit across the closet door and I steeled myself for whatever was coming next. I prayed the police came before he finished the job he'd been bragging about doing for the past six months.

"I know you're in there, Rabbit." His pet name for me was my undoing. I sucked in a quick breath, and released a squeak of fear. "Come out, come out wherever you are. I just need to talk to you, Rabbit. That's all."

That's all, my ass. His "talks" were the reason I had decided to leave him. His talks always led to the reasons why I wasn't good enough for him. They led to the improvements I needed to make to myself in order to be worthy of his time. He loved me on his arm in public, but beat me and belittled me in private. I just wished he would go ahead and get it done, because the in between part was slowly killing me. He loved to emphasize all of his life lessons with his fists.

In the blink of an eye, he swung the door to the closet open and calmly walked in. He stopped in front of where I was crouched and just stood there. The silence was maddening. I just needed to gain some small advantage, some element of surprise so I could bolt and hope the cops were less than a minute away. I had no idea what he was thinking. He just stood still, facing perpendicular to me.

He took a step forward and I made a flash decision. I was going to bolt and hope for the best. I unmuted my phone, sprung up, and lunged towards the entrance. I clipped him on my way by and he fell off kilter, but didn't stay that way for long. I could hear him growling behind me, but didn't dare stop to check his status. It was do or die time, literally. My deepest parts knew that if he got a hold of me, it was likely that he would end me.

I slammed into the door frame of our bedroom and catapulted myself into the living room. He was hot on my tail, breathing fire and screaming like a lunatic. You see, I knew his secrets. Not just the secret that he hits me, but his big secrets and he needed me to not tell anyone. He had his public image to uphold and people were depending on him for their livelihoods. Ha! What he didn't know was that his secrets were safe with me. I didn't want the spotlight. I didn't crave the attention like he did. I just needed to survive the night. That was plan A. Plan B was to get the hell out of the relationship.

He gained on me and decided to tackle me in the hallway at the top of the stairs. I went down hard and utter agony exploded all around me. This was it. He got me. But I wasn't going to make it easy on him. Nope, no fucking way. The sick bastard was going to pay for what he had done to me and countless other women and men. Men and women who were under the impression he could turn tricks with his dick.

He jumped on me. I screamed and started to kick and punch and try to gain purchase to knee him where it counted but I couldn't seem to feel anything around me. He pushed me towards the stairs and it all turned to liquid. I couldn't do anything but lie there and let him pummel me until I emitted an ear piercing scream, bolted upright and reached around me to grab him.

It was then I realized it was my high thread count sheets, duvet, softest pillows money can buy, and my ultra-lux mattress that I was lying on and not the floor, fighting for my life. Slowly, my pulse settled, my breathing evened out and I eased my way back into reality. I was safe. I was anonymous. He couldn't reach me here. It was my mantra and I kept repeating it over and over again until it was all around me and I could pretend to believe it.

Chapter 2

Frankie

I could feel the ocean at war with the wind. The hurricane they predicted, had now been downgraded to a tropical storm, but it still was coming in with gale force winds. I decided I needed to get out there and take some pictures before it was impossible to stand up. Then I would be able to refer back while finishing my painting. I grabbed my camera and ran outside, in enough of a hurry to completely forget that I was wearing only a tank top and bikini bottoms.

The wind instantly whipped my crazy, red hair around my face, completely obliterating my ability to see clearly and that's when it happened. I crashed head over heel, or ass over teacup, take your pick. Neither accurately conveys the propensity with which I dove into the sand. He was on me in an instant. His kisses trying to take away the hurt and the sand, but all he ended up doing was drenching me in disgusting slobber and getting piles of gritty sand in my face. I opened my eyes to see him mere inches from my face, with his tongue hanging out at an odd angle, and a big, goofy grin on his face.

I heard a sharp whistle through the howling of the wind and turned my head to try to locate its source. My damn hair was once again swirling around like Medusa caught in a wind tunnel so I couldn't quite place where the sound had come from.

"Chuck, leave her alone buddy. Sit."

Chuck instantly obeyed and I swung around to try to get a lock on his person. I attempted to wipe the remains of Chuck's affection from my face but all I ended up doing was getting more sand in my eyes, nose and mouth. I collapsed back into the sand, completely giving up. This day just wasn't going to be a win for me. I began a silent inventory of what I must look like. Wild and crazy red hair? Check. Tiny white bikini bottom nearly showing all my neglected lady goods? Check. Face covered in sand and slobber? Check. Camera gone flying and most likely full of sand? Check, check and fucking check.

"Can I help you up?"

He reached out a strong hand to help me. I weighed the pros and cons of taking that hand and decided I had enough mortification to last me the day and grabbed a hold of his life line. He hauled me up like I weighed nothing and steadied me in front of him.

"Thanks," I said, keeping my head down and still trying to fight the elements to be able to clearly see this guy. I turned to Chuck, who was patiently waiting further instructions beside us, and scratched his ears.

"Ah shit. Now you've done it. He won't listen to a thing I have to say anymore. Beautiful women always top Chuck's priority list."

I searched the sand for a reply while feeling my cheeks ignite. I tried to take peek at this stranger standing here in front of me, but my hair was once again on the move preventing me from being able to see much. I wish had the fore site to have tied it back. The thing was, my hair was my shield. It protected me from the glare of strangers and the speculation that I hated to endure. All I could make out thanks to my hair and the glare of the sun was that he was tall, and a guy. I tried to wipe the sand from my face with my tank, but it seemed useless. I was doomed to be completely embarrassed.

"Well, sorry I ran over your dog. I better get moving if I'm going to get a few shots in before the storm gets too strong to stay out in." I made to walk around him when he grabbed my arm. I looked back over my shoulder and tried not to show him the fear that always slept beneath my surface when someone touched me. He must have seen it as he dropped my arm and made quick work of disarming me with a charming smile.

Now that I was facing the opposite direction I had a clear view of the masterpiece in front of me. Chestnut brown, curly hair topped a tall frame. He had a rugged and refined face with warm, brown eyes and long glorious eyelashes. A dusting of stubble lined a defined jawline and that gorgeous head sat atop a body that an artist could gaze at for days upon days.

"I should be thanking you. Once Chuck gets a notion unto his pea brained head, he is focused on being on task until his mission is complete. You saved me a 3 mile run in the sand. I hate running in the sand and I hate running in the sand at the onset of a hurricane even more."

The wind chose that moment to pick up speed and become threatening. I sighed inwardly. I guess my pictures would have to wait. My memory would have to get me through today. I needed to paint the turmoil happening outside but always liked to have a reference point to come back to.

Suddenly, the storm took a violent turn and in the not so far distance, lightning and thunder joined the howling wind adding another element of danger to the already menacing storm. Chuck whimpered and I reached down to hopefully assure him he would be fine. As if the Gods had some part in how my life was just going to keep on throwing me curve balls, there came a crashing from behind me and we both turned to watch my deck furniture lift up with the wind and crash into one of my windows. Damn, why hadn't I tied it down? I was such a scatter brain and just getting used to being out here on the ocean on my own. Now what was I going to do?

"Ok, Red. Here's what's going to happen. We're going to run like mad back to what I am assuming is your house and get you and Chuck inside. Then I'm going to tie down your furniture and safety this house as quick as I can." He began to walk us towards my house. Shit. This cannot happen. Why was I always getting myself caught up in this drama?

"It's no use arguing. I can see it written all over your face that you don't like that idea and I know I'm a complete stranger, but you need help and what kind of man would I be if I just turned and left you here? And besides, Chuck here is a wimp of the finest kind. He needs you to offer him shelter before he loses his mind and pulls another runner. Let's get moving."

"Are you always this bossy?"

"Yup, better get used to it. For the time being, we are stuck together, so let's get a move on, Red."

"Stop calling me Red."

He just ignored me and dragged me onto my deck, shoved me and Chuck inside and slammed the back door. I was too shocked by this to do anything at the moment. He began stacking the chairs together, all the while dancing around the broken glass. I shook myself out of my near panic attack, ran and grabbed some towels and got to work. I ran to the storage room and found bungee cords and my broom and ran back to the door where he was still attempting to fight the wind and rain and get my deck secure. I passed him the cords and then joined him on the deck, trying to sweep up the broken glass.

"Back inside sweetheart. I can handle this."

I ignored him. I needed something to focus on or else having him in my space, coupled with the storm was going to freak me out so badly I wouldn't come outside for weeks.

"This is my house and I am in control of it, so step aside while I sweep up this glass before you cut your feet open and we have to drive you to the hospital in this storm. 'Cause hear me when I say, I will just dump you at emerg and keep on driving."

He stared at me for a second and I could have sworn his mouth was deciding whether to laugh or yell at me. He was saved from having to make that decision by a loud thunderclap, a bolt of lightning and then the pouring rain started coming in sideways. I quickly swept up the glass while the hot stranger finished securing the chairs and table.

"Do you have any plywood?" he yelled.

"What's plywood?"

He rolled his eyes as best he could in the storm. "A large piece of wood to board up the window until you can get it fixed."

"Oh, yes, the previous owner has hurricane supplies in the shed."

He bounded off the deck and fought with the shed door while trying in vain to keep the rain off his face. Chuck was frantically barking and pacing around the back garden door while simultaneously turning in perfect circles.

My rescuer came back with two pieces of wood, a hammer and some nails and got to work boarding up the broken window and my other back window while he was at it. I paused and took a minute to admire him while he had his back turned to me. His hair was soaked but his chestnut curls on top still resisted being flattened. A feature that I was all too familiar with on my head of hair.

His shirt was plastered to his body and from what I could make out, the body underneath was phenomenal. Toned muscles, lean, tall legs. He clearly was into staying fit and was genetically gifted from birth. And it was clear, someone had raised him to be a gentleman. Not many complete strangers would help someone in the middle of a huge storm that was predicted to last a good twenty-four hours.

"Are you gonna stand there ogling my assets or help me by holding these boards while I nail them in?"

"I wasn't-"

"You were, but I kinda liked it, so either carry on or come here and help me."

Mortified, I marched over to the windows to help him finish. He hammered the boards in and turned to me with a grin oozing dimples and charm. "Ok, that should hold you fine until tomorrow. I can call someone to come out for you to have it replaced? Just let me know. He strode to the door, pulled it open against the torrential rain and ushered me inside.

He reached down to calm Chuck and in the process, dripped water all over my floors. "Sorry," he said. He reached down to the hem of his shirt to what looked like, lift it off over his head.

"What are you doing?"

"Do you have a dryer? Can I just give it a quick dry before I head back out into the rain?"

"What would be the point? It's just going to get wet again."

"True, but it would give me more time here with you." He grinned a boyish grin that I was sure had gotten him all sorts of places in life. "My name's Hardy, by the way." He held out his hand and I just stared. How had this happened? This was my private island. No visitors. He needed to go.

I shook his hand and then promptly dropped it. "I think its best if you just head out now before the storm really gets going."

"Yeah, I guess you're right. Well, it was nice to meet you even though we haven't really met. I never did catch your name"

I just smiled. "So, thanks for helping me. I need to get going."

"Where are you going in this storm?" he asked.

I started to panic and began my horrible habit of scratching at my arms. I frantically looked around. Anywhere but into his eyes.

He reached out to still my hands and I stepped back to avoid his touch. "Hey, it's ok. I'm going now. Don't worry." He smiled and turned to grab Chuck. I looked down at my forearms and saw the angry red marks and wrapped my arms around my waist to avoid him seeing the results of my near panic attack.

A loud crack of thunder made me jump. "You'd better hurry. It's coming down good now, but looks like it's going to get much worse."

He grabbed the doorknob and looked back over his shoulder. "Are you going to be ok? I'm not really feeling good about leaving you here all alone. Is there someone coming home soon?"

"No. No one else but me. I'll be fine. I actually love storms."

"Riiight. Me too, but not being caught out in one. I better go." He grabbed his shirt from the floor, swung open the door and raced outside, Chuck right on his heels. He turned to look back at me and through the rain, I could see a sadness that mirrored mine in his brown eyes. He half waved and ran off with his dog on his heels and I couldn't help but feel a strange sense of loss.

I turned back to my easel, grabbed a brush, dabbed on the blue and got lost in the storm.

Chapter 3

Hardy

What the hell just happened? I'm trying to wrap my head around the past thirty minutes but my dumbass brain can't get past what she looked like soaking wet, from head to toe, wearing not much more than a see through tank and bikini bottoms. Fuck, I nearly threw her over my shoulder and hauled her off caveman style into her bedroom to have my way with her. Except, I kinda think she wouldn't have taken kindly to that and there was the issue that we had only met minutes before.

Fuck, and now, here I was, running in a hurricane, down the beach to my car, with a hard on and blue balls reminding me every stride at how long it's been since they've seen any action. I hate running on the beach and I don't know anyone who wants to run in a downpour, but I think it may be just what I need to get that redhead out of my system. Unfortunately, I needed to get my training cranked up a notch. I was getting soft and that wouldn't do me any good on the job. It looked like a long summer of running on the beach, rain or shine was all the excitement my immediate future held.

I finally reached the parking lot and cursed the day I thought getting a dog would ease the loneliness. Especially the long haired chicken shit, mutt spinning around my feet right now. There was no way he was going willingly into the bed of the truck and I had nothing to cover up my passenger seat inside.

"Shit, Chuck. You gotta lock that shit down if you're sitting up front. No shaking, no crying and absolutely no cowering like a baby in my lap this time." I gave him my best Caesar Milan stare and tried to mind meld him into understanding how much my baby meant to me. It would be weeks before I would be able to get the wet dog smell out of her, let alone hours of polishing his dog goo out of the passenger side.

I found an old sweatshirt and laid it down on his seat. He hopped up and immediately attacked the sweater, spinning around, bunching it up, shoving it over until he had it just right, which meant, shoved to the corner and not touching him in the slightest.

I didn't have time to care, as the rain was coming down so hard, it had become painful, considering I was still shirtless. I hopped in, reached over and grabbed the sweatshirt, tried to dry off and threw the truck into gear and took off like the devil himself was on our tail, all thoughts of an attractive red head pushed to the back of my mind.

Chapter 4

Frankie

The thunder booms and lightening shoots through my room making me bolt upright in my bed. I slow my erratic breathing and try to get some sort of hold on my nerves. I look at my clock to see that it's one in the morning and the storm hasn't calmed much at all. In fact, it might have gotten a little worse.

I think about Hardy suddenly. I hope he made it back to his car and is somewhere dry and warm. I let myself linger on him a while longer than I normally would. His smile. Those dimples were the cutest things I had ever seen. He must have been an adorable baby. What the hell? I raised my fingers to my face to feel an actual smile lingering there. Ok, I wasn't going to get back to sleep if I kept thinking about him. About his tall body. About the glorious peek I got had gotten at his abs of steel.

Another clap of thunder and I realized sleep just wasn't going to happen. I didn't have a t.v. and I wasn't sure that the power would stay on anyway. I decided to take advantage of my ocean view and sit and watch the storm from the snippets of light that came and went.

My mind drifted back to Hardy and then the inevitable slide to Patrick. My body gave an involuntary shiver at the thought of his name. I had left him in the middle of the night with my friends as accomplices in order to escape the prison sentence that was being his fiancé. George and Sam were the only two people in the universe who knew where I was and somehow, I was going to have to make sure it stayed that way. I had no room in my life for someone like Hardy, even as a friend.

I sighed. Memory lane was a winding road where I could easily get lost. I needed to steer clear of the memories and focus on creating a small, quiet existence here at my beach house. I could only stay here for a month or so. I had to keep moving around so I would be less likely to be found by him. Maybe I would get a dog. Chuck seemed like a great dog. Oh God. And here I went again. Thinking about Chuck led me to thinking about Hardy which led me back to the reasons I couldn't allow myself to think about Hardy. Stupid, damn thinking circle.

I got up at the next boom of thunder and wandered into the kitchen to put the kettle on the stove to boil. Tea and a book were the only way I was going to train my brain to keep focused.

While I waited for the water to boil, I sent a text to George. Since marrying Finn, she had taken to staying up late at night. Finn was an actor and worked at all hours of the day and was a natural night owl. George, not so much, but usually spent a lot of time with Finn on the set of whatever movie or tv show he happened to be working on. This wasn't because she was needy. It was because Finn was the most attentive and adorable husband. He wanted George with him all the time and as she was a writer, she could work anywhere. George wasn't always so on board with being with him all the time, but gave into him because she loved him equally as much. Add to that, they were having a baby and Finn's next step will be to just put a GPS tracker on George, as well as a heart monitor and possibly a fetal monitor for good measure, so it was easiest to just stay close to him.

George replied instantly. I guess it was only ten in LA.

> Hey lady. What's up? Isn't it like one there?

Can't sleep. U?

> On set w/Finn.

> Hey, Sam and I r thinking of heading out there. What does three weeks look like for u?

Finn ok with that?

> Eye Roll

I pretty much have zero engagements on the horizon.

> K. I will text u r flights and details ltr. U ok?

Yeah, just missing you.

> Miss you too. Gotta run. Baby needs to pee.

K. Luv ya.

> Luv u too.

My kettle started to whistle and I ended the texts and settled in for a few hours of reading and wondering where I went so wrong and how I could dig myself back out of this lonely place I now inhabited.

I woke up feeling restless and full of useless anxiety. A week had passed since the night of the storm, but it had left me with a ton of issues running through my mind. There was only one activity that I knew that could help ease these feelings and so I dragged my butt out of bed and dressed for a long, strenuous run on the beach. Running has saved me over and over again. It had the ability to drive all negative thoughts from my head and leave it blissfully empty. Unlike most runners, I ran without music. Just pure peace. When I ran on the beach, it added the element of water into the mix and it was all I could do not to pull a Forest Gump and run forever. I hadn't run in a long time. I was afraid of being out there alone and of getting too far from the safety of my house, but my body knew it was time.

I slipped on my running gear, pulled my mass of hair into a bun and went to grab a quick banana before I headed out. Glancing out the back windows, I could see an amazing day was dawning. I sat on the deck, tied up my shoes, attached my running belt and sport band and performed my usual visual checks around me. Deep breath in, then out and I decided it was safe to go, kicked up some sand and began to forget the nightmares that had induced this state of panic to begin with.

One foot in front of the other. Repeat times a million. When I run, I zone out. Like, exist on another plane zone out. This would be why thirty minutes into the run, I finally noticed I had company. I screamed and once again, found myself sprawled flat out on the sand, but this time, instead of under a dog, I was underneath Hardy.

"Jesus Christ. Get off of me," I screamed at him. I was too freaked out to realize the level of panic that had set into my voice.

"I'm so sorry. God, so sorry. I'm such an ass." He rolled to the side and sat up. He was covered in sand too and looked completely adorable and completely horrified at the same time. He reached out to help me up and I quickly scrambled to upright myself without his help.

"It's ok. I'm sorry I screamed. See ya." I began to get the hell out of there. I had suffered seven fitful sleeps thanks to him. I could not get that sweet head of brown curls out of my own head. And it looked like that affliction was going to stick. He picked up running beside me again.

"Hey, um, I don't do running partners."

"Ok."

"Yeah, so, um, see ya."

"Sure, see ya." And then he fell in behind me and continued running. Great. Now he was behind me, staring at my ass, which had severe panty lines, and what I am sure, jiggles that would remind a guy of jello like substances. I wasn't sure what to do. If I stopped, he would most likely plow into me again, but if I didn't stop, he would continue to be behind me and I wouldn't be able to focus. So, in order to avoid having him draping himself all over me again, I just shook it off and kept running.

What became glaringly apparent, quite quickly, was that he had just began his run when we collided, and I was nearing my turnaround point. I was becoming winded and needed to quickly figure out what my options were at this point.

Come on Frances. Suck it up and just talk to him and get him to understand striking up a friendship with you was pointless.

I saw my turnaround point up ahead and just decided to make a wide arc, wave goodbye and continue on home. Except, once again, the fates of fuck up Frankie took control. They had other plans for me. The fates thought torture by hot guy was in order and today was my day. I turned, waved to him without looking back and that was my mistake. I zoned out the whole way home thinking he had continued on in his initial direction. Nope. He scared the shit out of me once again when I stopped. He had followed behind me the entire time.

"OK, you're bordering on creepy stalker, Hardy." I put my hands on my hips for added emphasis. It was my I mean business pose.

"Not stalking you. I just wanted to make sure you made it back ok. Now that I see you have, I will take my creepy ass away from you, your royal highness." He turned to go and the wars within me started. Today, it was kindness' turn to win.

"Wait, I'm sorry. I just don't do anything in pairs. I'm kind of into solitary. Like, if I was in jail, I would cause shit just to go to the shoe."

He smirked. "The shoe? You've been watching Orange is the New Black, haven't you?"

I laughed. "I don't watch t.v."

His eyes bugged out and his mouth hung wide open. It always felt good to stun people with that little tidbit of info about me.

"So, how do you pass the time?"

"I paint. And read. And that's about it."

He suddenly reached up with his hand towards my face. I felt myself flinch and my head sidestepped his hand. He stilled and looked me in the eye. His green eyes were hypnotizing. I reminded myself that not every man hit women. I tried to communicate with him via our eyes, letting him know, he could finish whatever his plan was with his hand. I had to get used to people being near me again.

His hand continued its journey, heading behind my ear and landed on the loose bun I had pulled my hair into. He grabbed a hold of the elastic holding the whole pile together, gave it a few tugs and my swirling mass was released back into the world. He let his hand fall, the whole time, keeping the connection between us through his eyes.

"I missed your crazy hair," he said. "I haven't been able to get it out of my head all week."

Mesmerized, I just continued to stare into his face as my hair took back its freedom and began to fly all around my face. "It's beautiful." He caught a piece of the offending strand that wouldn't leave my face alone. He shook himself, snapped out of the daze he seemed to be in and smiled his oh so sweet, dimpled up smile.

"Well," he said. "See you soon, Red."

And with that, he spun around, put his headphones back in and took off running back the way he came.

Chapter 5

Hardy

What the hell was I thinking? I clearly wasn't thinking with my brain, but with my dick. I saw her and instantly, like being pulled by a magnet, ran towards her. What I didn't expect was her fear of me. Something had happened to this woman that had her scared of either me, or just men in general. I sure hoped it wasn't just me. Something about her was drawing me in, leaving me with feelings I hadn't expected to ever feel again.

I had been restless all week after our strange first encounter. I couldn't focus and every time I thought I saw her, my stomach did a stupid little dip when I realized it wasn't her. And then today, when I did see her, I crashed landed on top of that lovely body, scaring the shit out of her. Topping it all off, I really did a good impression of a creepy stalker.

It was that hair. I couldn't resist its pull on me. What the hell? I even reached out and touched it. Taking creepy stalker to the next level. The strange part was, I didn't care. I hadn't felt like touching anyone in the past five years, and suddenly, an accidental dog versus girl collision had me yearning for more.

It looked like I had a new running partner whether she wanted it or not. I had absolutely no problem following that lovely little ass around the beach all day. Kind of like dangling a carrot in front a rabbit. No clue if I would ever catch it, but I decided then and there, I was going to give it my best shot.

Chapter 6

Frankie

We established a similar pattern in the days that followed. I started out running, he joined me, we ran single file and then we separated. Most of the time, Hardy didn't have much to say, but sometimes he indulged himself with a running monologue. Then came today. Today he was different.

He was waiting for me outside my deck instead of joining me where he normally did and instead of his charming, dimpled smile, his face reflected the stormy sea we were running alongside.

"Hey," I said. "You're here."

"Let's run," he said. And then promptly did just that. He ran. But this time, he was the leader. I could barely keep up to him and after thirty minutes of hard running I needed to stop.

"Hardy, I'm turning around. See you tomorrow?" I stopped and faced the ocean bent over at the waist with my hands braced against my knees, feeling like a ton of bricks were pushing on my lungs. I decided to just walk back and take it easy. I took a few steps toward home and then heard him. He was barely speaking above a whisper, but I could hear him like he was yelling in my ear.

"Tell me your name."

I inhaled and wasn't sure exhaling was in my future. We had a good thing going, and now he had to go and ruin it by wanting to know my name. Everything would change from this point on. He was a man of honour. He couldn't know who I was and not tell someone. It was the someones who could hurt me and I needed to do everything I could to avoid them finding me. My name wasn't exactly a household name, but in certain circles, it was known and more so, the man I was avoiding was pretty much known everywhere.

"I can't tell you that, Hardy."

He stared at me with emotions running wild across his face. Like a slot machine they spun on until they landed on the winner. Pain. He slowly walked toward where I was rooted. I couldn't move if another hurricane force wind came upon us there and then. I felt like if I broke our stare down, I would feel the pain of it for a really long time.

"Why?" he whispered. I could hear him clearly now that he was standing just a foot in front of me. "I need to hear it. I need to know your name."

"Why?" I echoed his words back to him. "Why does it matter? What are we doing here, Hardy? We're just running. That's it. We don't need to know anything about each other, we just need to run."

"How long are you just going to run, Red? How long until you let me know you? I've been here. Every day for the past two weeks, running behind you, but I'm done with running behind you." He began to close the space between us until he was breathing my air. "I'm done waiting for you to give me a piece of you. I want it now." He lowered his voice and began to lean in. "Give. Me. Your. Name."

I had huge personal space issues. He was pushing every limit I had and it terrified me. I felt a tear start to trickle down my face. We were frozen, at a standstill. One of us had to move first and I realized I was actually afraid his move would be to walk away. Something woke up inside of me at that realization. Being alone was beginning to be pretty damn lonely.

"Frances, but my friends call me Frankie." I whispered the words he was looking for and then I promptly turned and ran like the track star I once was, all the way back to the safety of my house. Away from Hardy. Away from the feelings he was bringing to the surface.

As I reached the stairs to my deck, I paused and looked behind me. Off in the distance I could just barely see him. He was standing there as still as a statue. As if the wind or anything nature could throw at him would never take him down. I could sense his resolve from this distance and the familiar panic within began to rise up. I quickly ran inside, locked the door behind me and slid down to the floor trying to calm my nerves. I couldn't do this. A relationship wasn't what I could handle right now. God, I was such an idiot. Why did I give him my name? He could search the internet and find me there.

I stayed on the floor in that position for a while. My breathing eventually slowed and my mind took back control of the roller coaster that it was on. I reached for my cell laying on the side table and swiped it on. Five missed texts and one missed call. I opened the texts first and saw they were all from my friends Sam and George.

The panic started to rise again as I read their urgent messages. He was back. And he was looking for me. I once again controlled my breathing and typed out a quick reply.

Ok. Keep me posted.

I got an immediate reply from Sam.

> Have you not listened to your voice mail? Frankie, call us then we can three way.

I called up my voice mail and listened as Sam outlined how my violent ex-fiancé had been stalking her and George. They were both ok as they were well protected. George had Finn, who had security up the whazoo after their own private stalking experience last year. Sam just had her own security being all super famous and shit.

It felt so good to hear her voice. I really missed my best friends. They were my sisters and a girl couldn't go too long without them. I sent them both a quick reply that I was fine and would call later, then decided to take a quick shower and think about my options.

I woke up the next day and took off for my run. Except, when I hit the point where Hardy usually met me, he wasn't there. I refused to analyze why this made me sad and continued on my regular path. The same for the next day and then the next. When I returned from the third day's run where Hardy hadn't met me I decided I had finally succeeded in pushing him away. The only problem was, I felt like shit.

I came here to find peace. Not jump into the bed of the next guy who turned my crank. I needed to snap out of it and be thankful he had taken the hint.

I was about to take a shower when there was a knock on the back door. I froze. I wasn't expecting anyone and that familiar panic started to rise up. I crept to the door and gave my head a shake. If he had found me, he wouldn't be walking up and knocking on the door, Frankie. Jeez, get a hold of yourself. I took a deep, cleansing breath and opened the door.

"What the hell are you doing here?"

He was dressed in a loose pair of jeans and a tight long sleeve t-shirt. His mop of hair was wet. He must have either just taken a swim or came fresh from a shower. My mind was suddenly filled with visions of Hardy plums, dancing around in my head. I barked out a laugh at my dirty imagination and instantly locked that shit down. I turned the laugh into a discreet cough and plastered a serious expression on my face.

He looked at me with a mixture of concern and fear. "Can I come in?"

"Hardy, look, I'm really kind of busy." He didn't seem to really hear me or I guess he hadn't needed me to answer that question, as he pushed by me and made himself at home on my couch. "What do you think you're doing?" I asked.

"Making new friends. My therapist said it would be good for me. So, Frankie, what do ya say? Want to make my therapist happy and be my friend?"

I stared at him. He was too damn cute for his own good. He was sitting there, looking at me, his smile wide enough to make that gorgeous dimple appear. "I was just about to take a shower," I said.

"Don't let me stop you," he countered. "I'll do my best not to think about you, naked, in the shower."

Heat flooded my cheeks, but for some reason, other than screaming and pushing him out the door for that comment, I smiled back. He was charming and funny, and undeniably hot. It would be rude to push him out the door just at this moment. Hm, two could play at this game. Before I could find myself even more embarrassed, I made a beeline for the bathroom, calling to him over my shoulder. "OK, make yourself at home. I'm not the type of girl who takes an eternity in the shower. Be back in a few."

I ran from the room and made a beeline for the bathroom. In record time, I had washed and combed my hair and taken away the sand and grime that covered me from my run.

I quietly snuck back into the living room to sneak a peek at him. He was standing and facing the picture window, gazing at the ocean. He was tall, around six foot three. Long slender legs and broad shoulders, perfect for carrying heavy loads around. His light brown hair was cut short all over, except for the locks at the top he let grow longer. They were starting to dry and his adorable curls were sticking up all over. His stance suggested he was stressed about something. He had his legs spread and he was leaning his forehead against the glass, seemingly deep in thought. I felt like I was intruding on a very personal moment he was having with himself. Not wanting to disturb him, I backed up a few steps and loudly propelled myself forward. "I'm back. All showered up and everything." Jesus, I was an idiot, but I couldn't help myself. I wasn't good with men and it seemed with Hardy, I was possessed by my sixteen year old self.

He turned around and for a brief moment, something akin to utter desolation passed through his eyes, but it was gone before I knew it.

"You need to password protect your phone."

"What! Why were you on my phone?"

"Don't worry. I just programmed my number into and called you so I have yours."

He looked at me like that was no big deal. I sputtered and tried to think of something to say, but I was so wound up, nothing came out.

"Red, breathe. I promise that was all I did. I swear."

My breathing slowed and I realized it might be a good thing to have one local contact to call if I needed help in a hurry. I smiled and tried to let it go. I needed to start to let people in if I was ever to come back to life.

"So," he said. "What do you want to do? Want to play Twenty Questions?"

Despite my anxiety at having him here, I laughed. "That's my best friend George and her husband Finn's favourite get to know ya game. And, I think I'll pass, thanks. Why don't we start at me getting you a drink, since it looks like you're planning on staying? But just so you know, I've got lots of plans today and don't really have much time for talking."

He raised an eyebrow at my more than obvious lie. "Drink it is then. I'll have whatever you're offering."

"Well, it's going to have to be water. I don't have anything else to offer. Kind of off alcohol these days." I made a mental note, that if I was really going to go through with this friend thing, I would have to have drinks and snacks hanging around.

"Water is perfect, Red."

"I've told you my name now. You don't have to keep calling me Red." I turned around to give him his bottle of water and jumped. He had somehow snuck right up behind me without me knowing.

"I like Red. It suits you." He reached out and tucked a piece of my crazy hair behind my ear.

I was getting really nervous or hot and bothered or an anxiety inducing combination of all three. I couldn't tell, but still, I needed to put some space between us. Either he didn't notice or didn't care. He stayed put, boxing me in and continuing with his staring thing.

"Red. Like fire. Like heat. Like danger." We were in a trance. I couldn't tear myself away from his eyes. They held mysteries somehow more entrenched than mine. This man, standing here, touching my hair, talking to me in a low, sexy voice about how dangerous I was, held me. I couldn't stand to look away. Thankfully, he was still in control and broke the connection with a small shake of his head and took a step backwards looking just as shook up as I felt.

"Where have you been lately? I haven't seen you running in the past few days."

"Miss me?"

"No." I practically yelled that at him. "Just, that I've gotten used to you running behind me and it felt different without you there. You're a good pacing partner."

He once again began to close the space between us. "Good pacing partner? Come on Red, you never even acknowledge I'm there when we run. What happened to not running with a partner? Admit it, you actually missed me and you're too proud to say it."

I instantly became outraged at his completely on the mark statement. No way in hell I was letting him know that. "What the hell are you talking about? I set the pace, you push me to keep it going. That's how we work. I've been all over the place this week. I can't keep my running steady."

He raised one perfect, chocolate brown eyebrow. "Say it."

"Say what?"

"Say you missed me."

"I so did not and can you please step back. I have personal space issues and right this moment, you're pushing my limits."

"Am I? Good. I intend to push your limits a little each day, Frankie. I think you like it. I think you need me to set the pace. Whatever killed that little light inside of you, I'm here to let you know it can come back."

I inhaled sharply. "What the hell are you talking about? When did this-"I waved my hand back and forth between us, "turn into some sort of challenge? I never asked you for anything Hardy."

"Why not? Why aren't you asking me for anything?"

And here come the waterworks. I hadn't cried over the lost hopes and dreams I had in quite a while. Who was this man making me feel everything I had worked so hard to push away?

The tears were cascading down my face and I was powerless to stop them. His fingertips traced their path down my face, cupping my jaw on either side of my mouth. What was I doing? This was exactly the thing I had been trying to avoid since our paths collided on the beach.

Hardy looked just as terrified as I must have felt and I wondered once again, what secrets he was harbouring. "Frankie?"

"Yes?"

"I need to kiss you now, baby. And I promise, I'll go slow, but I need to do this. I have no idea what's happening with us, but I just need to kiss you. Please, please don't stop me 'cause I'm not sure I will have the courage to give this another try."

"Hardy," I took in a huge breath that came out more as a sob. "I don't think I can. I, I-." I was in a fight for control. My stupid, obnoxious brain. My brain that thought it knew better than anyone else what it was I needed to do to protect myself. It wouldn't let my heart just get a win for once. My heart was hurting, physically, it actually needed Hardy to kiss me so bad, but my stupid brain kept telling my body to brake. And it had my final hospital stay on repeat in my mind.

"I don't know-"
He didn't bother with words. He just choose right then and there to push my brain out of the way and tackle my heart. His lips crashed into mine and took over my thoughts, invaded my personal space and erased my nightmares. One simple kiss. Except, there was nothing simple about it. It was so complex and layered it could be my famous seven layer nacho dip.

It was in and out, it was up and around, it was everywhere and nowhere. He grabbed me behind my head and locked me in position. He had gotten wise to my ways and made sure I wasn't able to run. With his other hand, he was calming me like he would a scared animal who could bolt at any moment. He was softly stroking me up and down my arm and occasionally slipping around my waist to gently massage my back.

He tilted his head to gain better access to my mouth and I found myself tilting with him to give him what he needed. It was then, he kicked the kiss up in high gear. And then nothing. He just stopped.

"I'm sorry, Frankie. I shouldn't have done that."

I lifted my hands to my lips and tried to catch up with the storyline. "Why not?"

He started pacing, never a good sign. Pacing equals massive anxiety in my world. An emotion I know all too much about, but have no idea how to deal when displayed to me from the opposite perspective.

He walked over to me and grabbed a hold of my hands and smiled the saddest smile I had seen since looking in the mirror this morning. "Why not is a sad story for another day. I probably should be going. I left Chuck at home and he's probably going nuts trying to deal with his anxiety by now." He turned to go and I was still standing still, wondering, how I managed, on a beach all the way across the country, to find another person who could potentially be as messed up in the head as I was at the thought of making out with someone.

"Hardy." I called and he stilled before heading out. "Run tomorrow?"

He smiled and pulled out all the stops with those deep dimples of his. "Tomorrow, Red." And with that, he opened the door that he had only walked through thirty minutes ago, and took off in the direction he came from.

Chapter 7

Hardy

Once again, I'm leaving her wondering what the hell had come over me, except this time, it was a huge what the fuck?

I had been working for three solid days and had missed her like I'd never thought possible. While I was supposed to be focusing on saving lives, I was focusing on a fire of a different sort, a tiny, highly combustible firecracker named Frankie. The guys had all noticed something was off, but never in their wildest imagination would they think I had actually let a woman get under my skin.

That kiss had taken me by surprise just as much as it had Frankie. I hadn't kissed anyone since Sarah. I had messed around with a bunch of woman, but they all knew kissing was off limits. A kiss meant a lot to me and I wasn't going to lead any of those girls down a path where they thought they had any chance of developing anything beyond sex.

Something had happened when she opened her door. A shift inside of me that I wasn't expecting. My hands gripped the wheel tighter than normal and I had to force myself to relax. Easier said than done. I also had to process the reasons why I kissed her and then ran away.

I wasn't a fucking coward. It was a total douche move and I felt really bad about it, but not bad enough to turn around and fix it. I needed a break from whatever was happening and I needed to figure out if I was ready for the complications that surely came with me pursuing Frankie.

It was obvious something was lurking behind those eyes. A huge distrust, but also a shit ton of fear. That girl was running scared of something, but I would bet money on it being someone. If I knew how to work my damn computer, I would try doing an internet search on her, but for starters, I had no fucking clue what her last name was and I wasn't sure I wanted to invade her privacy. I hoped she would tell me in time.

In time. I guess I had made my decision. Pursuing her it was.

I pulled into the driveway of Sarah's dream home. We were going to raise our family here, but the universe had other plans. I sat in my truck waiting for something to hit me. Anything that told me it wasn't time to move on, but there was nothing. I wasn't much for signs, but a little something would be good.

I sighed and leaned back against my seat and closed my eyes, but all I saw was a sprinkle of freckles across the sweetest little nose. Fine features and that flaming, wild hair that I knew, once uncovered, would match her fiery temper. Chuck sealed the deal when he came skidding across the driveway, bounding up onto my car. That damn dog. I smiled. "Chuck, you just may be on to something buddy."

Chapter 8

Frankie

I took off the next morning, excited for my morning run and maybe, if I was being honest with myself, excited to see if that gorgeous face would meet me halfway. Sure enough, he was there, this time with Chuck and we fell back into our usual rhythm. Me in the lead, Hardy bringing up the rear, Chuck, darting all around us, into the ocean and out.

I listened to Hardy talk to his dog as we ran, wondering, how the hell he could carry on a conversation and make it mean something while running along the beach, even if it was to a dog. I develop asthma during every run and used it as my excuse mostly to keep quiet. It might be a figment of my imagination, but I'll never admit to it.

He talked about his childhood and his family and instructed Chuck on the ways of the world and sometimes I felt as though he forgot I was even there.

We returned back to my beach, exhausted and wheezing, well, I was anyway. Hardy, as per usual, had barely broke a sweat. Just enough sweat to look like an Abercrombie model pretending to exert himself.

I caught him staring at me with his usual intense gaze.

"What," I asked?

"Nothing. Just thinking."

"Thinking about what?"

"Thinking about who did this to you."

And, the walls are back up. "What makes you think someone did something to me?"

"Frankie, I know that look. I see it often in my own bathroom mirror. You've had shit happen, it's there. Lurking behind the scenes. We've been running for weeks now and I've yet to see you laugh."

I struck a pose of righteous indignation. "I laugh. I'm funny. Are you calling me sad and boring?"
"What the hell, Red? I never said that."

I marched over to him pointed my perpetually pissed off pointer finger right in his face. "I laugh buddy. Did you ever think maybe, you're just not funny?"

He looked at me with a smug smirk I was so motivated to destroy. "Babe, I'm funny."

His smirk grew into a full-fledged, evil smile. "Babe." He slowly grabbed the finger I had waved in his face, popped it in his mouth, circled it with his tongue and slowly drew it back out of his mouth, letting it go with a soft noise, all the time, never losing eye contact with my eyes.

"That wasn't very funny," I whispered.

Still not having broken our eye contact, he returned his glorious, innocent smile to his face and pulled my hand out to the side. "No, it sure as hell wasn't. But when you least expect it, I'm gonna make you laugh and you'll eat those words and they will taste just as amazing as that beautiful, angry finger of yours you're always poking me with. And yeah, babe, every single sexual innuendo was intended there." And with that parting shot, he turned around and ran back the way he came.

I brought my offending, traitorous finger up to my cheek and willed the memories it invoked to disappear. I came here to find peace, to find myself, to get lost and to try to find a path back to the light where I used to live.

Maybe that path wasn't so straight and narrow like I had always planned. Maybe there could be space for another soul to walk with me. Or maybe I was kidding myself. I didn't know how to be with a man anymore. Patrick took that from me and gave me fear in return. And regrets. My life was currently one big pile of wishful thinking that I had chosen a different path when he was placed in my way. But I didn't and I have to spend my life living with the consequences of that guilt weighing me down.

I thought about what Hardy had said about me not laughing. Of course he was right. I struggled to bring the last time I laughed into my brain and it was getting tired heading back so far into the past. I'm pretty sure it was after I met Patrick and probably while hanging out with Sam and George.

Now that brought a smile to my face. I couldn't wait to see my friends. They were due to visit this weekend. I suddenly had an idea. I ran into the house, grabbed my phone and snapped a smiley selfie. Before I lost my nerve, I texted it to Hardy and immediately threw my phone across the room onto the couch as if it was on fire, and ran into the bathroom to shower and then get ready for my girls to come stay for the coming weekend.

I decided that if I was going to feed my friends, I would actually need to find a grocery store and get some food. My kitchen was looking pretty scary, what with the fridge being occupied solely by water bottles, and condiments. I couldn't live much longer on crackers and bagels.

The town was a small town with two stop lights and a handful of stop signs. The grocery store the next town over could be reached either via the coast road, or heading through town. It was a beautiful day, so I decided to head along the coast towards the store.

I spent some time trying to write a quick list in my car and then gave up and headed in to grab as much food as I could. I tried not to head out very often, so when I did need something, I bought enough to last me a good long while.

I quickly surfed through the tiny store and got nearly everything I thought I would need to host my two best friends for however many nights they were staying. Being that George was pregnant and married to overprotective Finn, I suspected they wouldn't be staying that long. But, stranger things had happened so I indulged myself and got piles and piles of food. The only thing I needed was meat and that required a stop at the local butcher shop. This would require me to head straight into the downtown core so I would have to drive up the main street and skip another lovely coastal drive. I neared the intersection of Main and Ocean Dr when I noticed a long line of cars stopped and waiting to get through.

"Wonder what's up?" I spoke aloud to myself. I totally needed a dog. I had to stop talking to myself and at least with a dog, people would assume that I was talking to it instead of looking at me like I had lost my ever loving mind.

I bet Hardy could help me find a dog. Wait, what? Since when did I ask strangers for help. I guess he wasn't really a stranger anymore. Just a man I ran alongside every day, oh and a man who could kiss my socks off. I didn't know much about him, but I did know he loved dogs and Chuck was the cutest dog ever.

As I neared the main point of congestion, I realized it must be a fundraiser for the fire department. There were firetrucks parked across the intersection and lots of people and firemen milling around talking and laughing and basically enjoying small town America. I pulled up to the fireman standing in the middle of the road and saw he had a boot in his hand and a really familiar dimple peeking out from under his ball cap.

I let my window go down and took in all that was Hardy Hanson before he had the chance to spot me. I had no idea he was a firefighter. I was so going to have to start paying attention while he talked when we were running. This was critical information I had missed. As I rolled up to him, I took in all that he was in his uniform. Tall, check. Fit? Check. Classically beautiful face with a pinch of ruggedness? Check and clearly now I had slipped into a cheesy romance novel, because I think my next mental description was swoon worthy? Checkity check check check.

I came to a stop and he stuck his head in. His eyes lit up and he brought out his A game smile, dimples and all.

"Hey Red," he whispered.

For some reason unknown to me, I felt a slow blush creep up towards my cheeks. I stuttered and tried to talk, but all of a sudden, Hardy's face being this close to me brought my intelligence quota down a few hundred points. I managed a weak, "hey," and tried to look anywhere but in those warm brown eyes of his.

"Got any spare change? We're collecting donations for a local family whose house burnt down last week. Anything you can offer is awesome. We're filling our boots and then spending the rest of the day rolling the coins and counting the cash. Later on there's a BBQ at the fire hall. You should come."

"Oh, I don't think so, but I can donate for sure." I reached into my wallet and pulled out the remaining cash I had in there and stuffed it in his proffered boot.

"Frankie, do you know how much you just stuffed in there?"

"Not really?"

"It looks to me to be around five hundred dollars. Are you sure?"

I smiled. He was so adorable and I must be losing my mind as the word adorable had only ever escaped my lips when it was directed at a baby. I mentally slapped myself to get it together and lock that shit down. "It's fine Hardy. I'm happy to help and this is probably the only way I can right now." A horn honked behind me and I could see a look of irritation flit across his face.

"Here, hold this." He shoved the boot at me and shoved half his body into the window and reached across me. He grabbed a pen from my console and on his way back out the window, grabbed my free hand. I was too stunned to question what in the hell he was doing and before I knew it, I was transported back to high school when I looked at my hand. An address was scribbled there and I felt a teenaged giggle bubbling around inside my chest. "It's the BBQ address. You should come. I'd really like it if you did."

The horns started honking again, but he completely ignored them. He stretched back in the window, got way into my personal space and brought his voice down low and whispered in my ear. "Come tonight, Red. Just take a step towards the light. No strings, no nothing. Just get out, meet some people who can surround you here and eat some burgers. And by the way, loved the smiley face text, but the jury's still out on you being funny." And before I could react to his being in my space, he softly kissed my cheek and disappeared from my window with a wink and a smile. A honk brought me out of my daze and I took off, never once letting my hand leave the spot on my cheek where his lips had connected with my skin. If I had been able to move my head in any direction other than straight North, I would have been able to see myself in the rear view mirror and what I saw would have given me another glimmer of hope that I had started to emerge from the fog. The ridiculous smile that was plastered there could have lit the way through the thickest of haze.

Chapter 9

Frankie

I unpacked my groceries and wandered aimlessly around my house finally ending up in front of my easel with a brush in my hand. I reached over, turned on my iPod and decided it's time to get lost in the paint. My brushes are an extension of my body and have always been the way I work through my problems. Well, they were until I met Patrick. I stopped painting for our entire relationship. He stifled my creative soul and pushed me farther away from my true self. The isolation he made me feel had damaged me nearly to the point of no return until one day, George and Sam staged an intervention. That was the day my world changed forever.

I closed my eyes and practiced pushing all those feelings out to sea, just like my therapist had taught me. When I felt settled, I opened my eyes and started. I painted without direction, just pure emotion. I went into the maze that was my brain and for the first time in a long time, wasn't afraid to get lost.

I suddenly noticed the light in the room changing and glanced out my picture windows that gave me a clear view of the ocean and beyond. I looked up at the wall clock and notice it's getting close to six o'clock. I'm exhausted from standing that long and painting but exhilarated from feeling my creative soul catch fire again.

I take a step back from my easel and smile. I painted the ocean and the shoreline. Along the shore there are two figures, running, single file. The leader, has her head turned and is looking back at the man following her. She isn't smiling but her face, what you can see of it, shows the world she knows him, knows he has her back, but in turning, she's letting him know, she needs him behind her. You can't see his face, but his head is tilted slightly to the left and you can imagine he's smiling and encouraging her on.

I plop down onto the couch and hold my head in my hands. Why the hell had I painted Hardy and I running? I did not even want to begin to examine the reasoning behind this painting.

My phone lights up as my eyes happen to be sweeping in its' direction. I grab it to distract myself from my internal issues and immediately see that the damn phone is no help in that regard at all. It's a text from Hardy. It starts with a picture of him and his boot and it's overflowing with money. Beneath it is a caption – *thanks for the donation, Red. The boot is full, now come get a burger and you can be full too.*

Groan

> *See, I'm a funny guy. Fun-gi on your burger?*
>
> *Say you're coming or these jokes won't stop.*

Fine. Please, God, stop. Be there in a bit.

I pull into the parking lot of the fire hall, yet again today, and instantly spot Hardy. He's taller than the rest of people milling about, but that's not why I can see him. It's the gaggle of women surrounding him.

I get out of my car and lean against the hood to observe the pack before Hardy can see me. He's never mentioned a girlfriend, or wife for that matter and it suddenly strikes me as odd that neither of us know all that much about the other.

I watch him man the BBQ and chat up the ladies with the ease of a practiced flirt. I don't blame them. He looks all kinds of hot in his uniform. I guess I've just never seen him around anyone other than me. One perky blonde in particular seems a little eager to get a burger from him. I'm about to push off my hood and wander over to him when I feel something so completely shocking I stop dead in my tracks. Shit, I'm jealous.

The fire only gets worse when she giggles and leans over to literally, peck him on the cheek and lift her left leg at the same time. It's like I just got transported back into the 1950's. Yup, there it is again. Definitely, all in jealous. Now what the hell was I going to do about it was the question.

I had yet another choice to make where Hardy was concerned. Pretend the jealousy wasn't there and continue our relationship, if you could call it that, on as it was, or acknowledge the feeling and try to understand why I'm feeling this way and see what comes of it.

While deciding, I started chewing on my fingernails, my worst habit ever. I couldn't kick it. I chewed when I was bored, but mostly when I was terrified. Hardy looked up and I accidentally, on purpose, stared right into his eyes. The jig was up. I was left with no options now that I had waited for so long. He had seen me and it was time to go bowling for bitches. Look out girls, queen B is in town and she's a little unstable and a lot unsure of herself, so you can bet that means all kinds of crazy shit hitting the fan at the fundraiser and somehow I knew, my red hair would be at the root of it all.

I held his eyes as I wandered towards the lineup and arched one eyebrow upwards, while tilting my head towards his adoring fans. He responded with an unrepentant grin and a sexy as hell chin lift in my direction.

I got into the lineup and tried to look unaffected. I discovered the ladies in the line had a tendency to stay and chat awhile when they reached Hardy, making the line intolerably slow moving. I finally reached the first station, the burgers, and politely declined the man who was offering them up.

"What, you don't want my burgers, sweetheart?"

Ugh, that word and his tone reminded me all too quickly of the reason I hadn't left the house much the past year. My ex had called me sweetheart, but it was always in a more condescending tone that most men would use. The firefighter standing in front of me used the same tone and was making my skin crawl.

"No, I don't, thanks," I replied using my best sorority bitch voice.

He raised his eyebrows and leaned back, placing his hand on his chest. "What? What's wrong with my burgers? Honey, ain't no better burger around."

"I'm sure you're correct in that assumption, but I came here today for something a little, um," and I lowered my voice to a whisper and leaned in real close so only he could hear, "bigger." I paused for effect. "And longer, if you know what I mean?"

I straightened up, turned and walked towards Hardy and the hot dog station. He had barked out a laugh, but was busy with Booby LaRue hanging over him. He looked up at me, smirked, winked, then went back to the bimbo.

I felt a strange stirring in my stomach and was fighting a full on smile. I stared at the ground and refused to look at anyone, or let the smile get free. I had no clue where that outburst had come from and I wasn't sure how it would be received. I moved forward, and when I came upon another set of boots across the table, I dared to look up into his eyes. I hadn't spoken to a man like that since college, and damn, it felt amazing. But now, I was concerned that I had offended a friend of Hardy's or worse, made myself another male enemy with my stupid mouth.

So, I opted for an upward glance, under the cover of my eyelashes to gauge the situation.

One my way up, I felt a finger settle below my chin and force my entire face up. My eyes finally followed and were met with a dazzling, full on dimpled, smile. "Babe that was the coolest thing I have heard spoken to Little Jimmy in a hell of a long time. You are the shit, girl."

I let out a breath and gave him a tentative smile, still unsure of how many people wanted to hurt me for mouthing off to one of their own. "Sorry," I huffed out. "He reminded me of someone I really want to forget. I'll have two hot dogs please, Hardy."

"Two? You're killin' me. I've never, in my life, met a lady that puts Jim in his place, then strolls past the burgers and orders two hot dogs after doing so."

"I love hot dogs, Hardy."

"Say that again."

"What? I love-"

"No, skip to the good part. Say my name again, Red. It sounds all kinds of amazing coming from your lips." I tried to look down, blushing furiously, but belatedly realized he still had two fingers planted firmly under my chin. "Say it," he whispered. "Give me something to know I'm on the right path."

I was sure that path should not lead to my door, but my damn heart had decided to take another lopsided step into the land of the living again today. Eyes still locked onto his with the grip of a Death Star tractor beam, I joined my heart and whispered back the word he wanted. "Hardy."

"Two dogs, coming up." He smiled, turned his back to me to grab them from the grill and returned with a shit eating grin that I couldn't resist smiling back to.

I grabbed the dogs, smiled like a lunatic in thanks and turned to leave. I had had enough testing out this new path for the day, but giggled to myself and turned back before leaving. "For the record," I paused to make sure I had his attention, "Hardy, I like hot dogs. A lot. And I prefer the foot long version."

His jaw dropped, then he howled in laughter and I turned to go, throwing a little something extra into my walk for his benefit. While heading back to my car, I noticed some glares being thrown my way by the bitches hanging all over Hardy when I arrived and smiled a private smile, knowing his laughter was for me alone. I hopped in and marveled at all that had happened over the past few weeks. Hardy Hanson. Who'd have thought getting run down by a dog would lead to me coming out of the dark and welcoming a bit of the light.

Chapter 10

Hardy

I saw her car pull in, but in no way was I going to let her know that. I had to play this exactly right in order to not scare her away, but damn, it was hard not to rush over and scoop her up.

I had been on hot dog duty for thirty minutes now, trying not to text her to see if she was coming, but letting it be her decision. The result felt like the Bachelorette show in the parking lot. Every single woman seemed to be out here tonight and they all seemed to have their sights set on me.

I didn't go out much so I guess they thought that if I was out, I was still single and ready to mingle. They couldn't be more wrong. I was definitely single, but only interested in mingling with one particular red headed vixen. And it looked like she may just be interested in mingling with me.

She got out of her car and leaned up against the door, pretending she didn't have her eye on me. It was getting hard to watch her out of the corner of my eye with all these woman yacking me up. Although, I could see she was definitely interested in what the bachelorettes were up to. Her eyes were narrowing and I could see the green eyed monster make a small guest appearance.

This could actually work to my advantage. I decided to roll the dice and engage with the ladies and see how she reacted. It was a dick move, but I was starting to get desperate. If I didn't get her off her car and over to the BBQ soon, she was going to change her mind and bolt. She must have come to some sort of conclusion, because she marched her cute little rear end to the end of the line, crossed her tiny arms over her chest, which enhanced her amazing assets, and proceeded to pout like it was nobody's business.

The line was moving interminably slow, but she finally got close enough that I could catch her eye without seeming too obvious. Her eyes caught mine and she gave me her best stink eye, and bingo. I knew I had a shot. She was jealous. This was more progress in twenty minutes than I had made in nearly three weeks. I should have tried this method sooner.

I saw Jim move in for the kill and tried my best to hear what they were talking about. Jim was a dick of epic proportions, but he hadn't realized that yet. In his mind, all the ladies loved him.

I could see him eyeing Frankie up and down and knew he was about to get burned by my Red. She might have been distant and uncommunicative with me for the most part, but I knew she had fire deep down in her soul. She had let it free a couple of times, but it looked like she was ready to play.

Just then, a particularly eager blonde leans over the table and asks for a hot dog. It sounds like Frankie got into it with Jimmy, but thanks to the blonde, I can't hear exactly what's said, right up until I hear her insult his manhood and I can't hold it back. Shit, she's good. I wish she would unleash some of that bitchiness on me. Seeing her all fired up has me completely turned on.

I bark out a laugh and quickly shift my eyes to the woman in front of me. She smiles and I kick myself for most likely laughing at something she said. I look over and catch Frankie's eye and wink. She rewards me with a cute half smile, fighting to become a full on grin and something stirs to life inside of me. It's time and this time, I'm not taking no for an answer.

Chapter 11

Frankie

The next day, I'm pacing up a mad storm and the sneaky little dust bunnies that multiply on my floors have totally met their match. I am anxiety personified. My girls are late. They should have been here by now. I anxiously check my watch and the wall clock for the thousandth time. I know they will be here any minute and it's getting hard to wait. I went from seeing them three or four times a week, to not seeing them very often and the need to see my best friends has been slowly killing me.

I fiddle around straightening things and try to read until I finally hear a car pull up into the gravel driveway. I jump from the couch, race outside slamming the door on my way by, and launch myself into George's open arms. Well, as much as I comfortably and safely can do without knocking her over. She's five months pregnant and kind of getting hard to wrap my arms around.

"George, you're crying."

"Of course I'm crying. I'm fucking full of hormones and just a breath away at all times from losing my shit. But more importantly, you're crying Franks. You know you don't cry, right?"

I reach up to feel the wetness on my face. "Yeah, well, a lot has changed in the past year and I've become a blubbering mess."

I am suddenly catapulted sideways and thrown so off balance I nearly fall into the pond at the side of the drive. "Sam." I breath a huge, freeing sigh. Everything will be fine now. Sam is here. Sam is our protector. The one who always has her shit together. Our glue. And damn, she's crying too. We're doomed. She pulls me to rights and grabs onto my arms and smiles. I don't let a lot of people in my personal space and she knows this. "You're touching me Franks. And you're not cringing. Nice job."

I grin and turn to lead them into the house, completely unable to wipe the silly smile off my face. I disowned my family a year ago when I left my fiancé after he tried to beat me to death. My parents had chosen him for me and weren't impressed when I left him, even though he left me, bloodied and beaten to within an inch of my life. Sam and George were my family now and it was so good to have them here with me. I didn't know how much I needed them until they pulled up.

I got the girls settled into their rooms and prepared a snack. I glanced at the clock and noticed it was ten. Shit, I had forgotten to tell Hardy I wouldn't be running today. I chewed my bottom lip as I debated running down the beach to find him. I decided against it. It would be too late now anyway. He would have figured out I wasn't coming by now, surely.

As if summoned by my thoughts alone, I look up to see an angry Hardy glaring at me through my garden doors. He raises one eyebrow and motions me outside. I walk towards the door, as if pulled by his insanely sexy tractor beam, yet again, and when I reach the door he opens it and yanks me outside.

"Hey, I've got company. What the hell are you doing?"

"Where have you been? I've been standing down there worried sick." He looks like an angry fish wife, glaring at me, hips on hands, eyes bugged out. I feel an unfortunate smile start to tug at my mouth. It's a bad habit I have. Finding uncomfortable situations kinda funny. I think it's a defense mechanism but I have never had the need to explore that reasoning until now.

"Do you find something about this funny?"

That was it. I burst out laughing. I've been so stressed lately and this seems to be the straw that broke my camel shaped back so to speak. I can't stop. And then I make the mistake of looking up at Hardy from my doubled over position. He still has his hands on his hips, but he is looking at me with a combination of horror, confusion and heat. Then, to make matters even worse, I find this look makes me start to cry. Jesus Murphy, I have simply lost my mind. At this very odd and unbelievably crappy point in time, I have decided I find Hardy both mind-blowingly sexy and extremely endearing and I want him, and that is so not something I can deal with sanely.

I tried my best to stop both the laughter and the tears and took a deep breath in. I happened a glance upwards and saw his focus had drifted past me and he was gazing intently now at something behind me. Turning my head around, I saw Sam and George, plastered up against the windows like toddlers looking at the ice cream truck. Their mouths were hanging open, their eyes were wide and round and they were wearing silly, huge grins on their faces with a tiny bit of drool on Sam's mouth. "Shit," I whispered to myself. I hoped they had half a brain and knew I needed them to stay inside. The last thing I needed was my friends playing matchmaker on me.

Of course, the Gods of Friends who Think They Know Best, weren't favouring me today and they sprang into action practically falling out the door on top of each other. Hardy jumped forward, pulling me out of their path of destruction. His hands traced my arms and landed on my wrists, loosely testing my stability. "You ok, Red?" The concern in his eyes almost had me back at the laughing phase, but I pulled myself together and shook off the feeling of impending doom.

"Yup. Fine, just fine." I pushed away from him, but he wouldn't let go of my arms. "Hardy, I'm fine."

Sam, unsurprisingly was the first to jump in. "Hardy? Why, I don't think we've been properly introduced. Frances, wherever are your manners?"
"What happened to your voice, Sam?" I asked.

George, my sane and normal best friend pushed Sam behind her pregnant belly and stuck her hand out to Hardy. "Hi, I'm George and this is Sam and we are very pleased to see Frankie has made a friend. It only took her a year, but she's always been a little bit on the slower side."

"Jeez, George. You're the best." I needed to get these two away from Hardy before they pulled out the high school yearbook pictures. Add to that, Hardy looked like he was contemplating multiple exit options and none of them would end with me just carrying on as if this whole conversation hadn't just happened. No, he needed to leave now and he needed to leave with a firm handshake and a "there is nothing going on between Frankie and I" lesson plan. The implementation of this plan was just going to have to be an exercise in finesse I wasn't sure I was within my abilities.

"Hardy, meet George and Sam, my two very best friends from LA. Ignore Sam, she thinks she's famous or something and is constantly pretending to be an A lister. George, is well and truly married to an A-lister and is also currently growing their child in her super cute womb." I took a breath and turned to the girls.

"Ladies, this is Hardy. My running partner and local firefighter. And he was just leaving, right Hardy?" I begged him with my best attempt at puppy dog eyes to take a hint and vamoose, but he just stood there. Probably because Sam and George each had a hold of one of his hands and were grinning like idiots.

Sam came back to life first. "Hardy. So do you live around here?"

"Y-"

"No," I jumped in. "He doesn't. In fact, I don't have any clue where he lives and so let's send him back there and he can let us know where it is when he gets there." There, problem solved. I could officially be classified as a lunatic and Hardy could get lost before the girls really got going and ended up giving him a facial and finding out his sign. What I hadn't planned for though, was Hardy. He smiled his stupid assed cute as hell smile, widened his stupid gorgeous runner's legs so he was stable and laughed his stupid, rich, deep amazing laugh. Damn, stupid, amazing Hardy. Damn you to hell. I was so not going to do this.

George decided to take a moment to remind herself she was a happily married woman and spoke up while discreetly closing her gaping mouth. "Frankie, have you lost your damn mind? Let the poor man speak. What has gotten into you?"

Hardy had finally managed to remove their tentacles from his hands. He had finally clued into the dangerous vibe of these three best friends, two of which were match making meddlers. He had the good sense to start to look worried and slowly planned an exit with his now shifty eyes.

I decided to step in and save both of us. After all, I did stand him up, leading him to my deck, which got us into this whole mess to begin with. "The girls are here for the weekend from LA and we were just about to catch up and have some quality girl time. I'm sorry I forgot to tell you yesterday. I won't be running for the next couple of days while they are here-"
"Yes we will," Sam jumped in. I looked at her like she had grown an extra head, for that extra loud mouth. "We could probably use a run, right George?"

"No, we could not Sam. I'm five months pregnant and even if I wasn't, I could never use a good run. Give the poor guy a break and say goodbye." George gave me a small smile and began the arduous process of dragging Sam away from Hardy. Just as she was about to claim success, Sam turned around and blurted out, "we're going to the Beach Bar tonight. You should come, Hardy. Frankie sings a mean karaoke."

Oh, she did not just say that. What was wrong with her? I did not need a social life and I certainly did not need Hardy learning any more about me. I had to put a stop to this train wreck now.

I grabbed his arm and turned him around and led him back off the deck. "So, sorry about my friends. They can be kind of crazy. They don't get out much."

"Frankie, it's fine. Stop stressing." My wild hair was once again flying in our faces. I startled when he gently reached up with a small smile and grabbed hold and cleared the space of it between us. "You're different today. I like it." And with that statement, he leaned in, softly kissed my lips and turned to go. Immobilized and completely unsure of myself, I stood once again, watching him go. He turned his head, smiled and said, "Might see you tonight. Can't wait to see what my little songbird can do with that mouth."

He immediately turned and started jogging up the coast, towards wherever it was he went after we finished our daily runs. Me on the other hand, well, I had turned into a zombie. Not the cold, dead, scary type. It seemed I was the alive, freshly implanted heart, blood pumping on the lookout for something zombie. Much less frightening to the general public, but terrifying to the person whose body it was occupying.

Chapter 12

Frankie

The minute I closed the door they pounced. I knew the discussion was inevitable, but was hoping for a small reprieve to gather myself. After all, I had just woken up from a long, cold slumber and found myself falling for a man I had no intention of falling for.

Sam went first. "So, here's how it's gonna go, Franks. We're going to grab this here wine," she held up a bottle in each hand, "George is going to grab those bowls of chips and you're just gonna march your pretty little ass back out on that amazing deck and park it. Then you're gonna spill every last drop of delicious goodness on that man and the reason you felt you had to hide his very existence from your two best friends. So, let's get on with it."

So, I got on with it. I started from the beginning, making sure not to leave one drop of juicy info out and finished up with how Hardy saves lives for a living and has a harem of married and unmarried tramps hanging on his every word, and I had no idea how to handle my jealousy when I was around them.

I finished talking and laughed at the look on their faces. I figured I had gone this far, I might as well finish. "So, I think I'm ready."

The best part about having the very best of friends was the unnecessary need to explain myself. These two were with me at the hospital when the ambulance brought me in. They held my hands, one on either side, when I had to labour to give birth to my son. My son, who was born 18 weeks early and severely injured due to his daddy kicking his head in. They were there when the p.r. person from my boyfriend's campaign came to the hospital to persuade me to keep quiet about the whole "incident" and finally they were there when I made the decision to go into hiding. They were my family, my everything, my support, but most of all, they were my legs when I couldn't walk away. And so, here they were, listening to me telling them I was going to be ok. I had found a tiny bit of light to shine on the tiniest of paths out of the darkness that I wore like a protective cloak around me. They just knew, that when I said I was ready, their job was done. My momma birds were going to watch all their hard work finally pay off. Their Franks was about to fly.

Wow, listen to me getting all sappy. These thoughts were barreling through my head like a train out of control. I gulped back a swill of wine and jumped up. "We're going out ladies. Don't bother getting too dressed up. I'm pretty sure jeans and t-shirts will do."

We rolled up to the Beach Bar in Sam's rental and already we stuck out like a sore thumb. Her white Mercedes was parked alongside trucks, jeeps, rusted out cars and hell, there were even a few bikes leaning up against the wall. I was thankful Sam had toned it down for the night, well, as toned down as she could live with and George being pregnant, meant she was sporting her usual yoga pants that she had decided to dress up with a tank and a pink cardi. I was wearing my uniform of skinny jeans and a flowing tunic with three quarter sleeves. Together, we linked arms and opened the door totally unsure of what was waiting for us, but more than ready to have some long overdue fun.

Loud, country music was pumping through the sound system so it made it hard to talk, but we held onto each other and made our way into the bar. It wasn't too busy yet, so we could choose our table. Sam took the lead, as per normal, and took us to a relatively secluded spot where we sat down and exhaled. First hurdle accomplished. The longer I was out of my comfort zone, the more anxious I was getting. I hadn't been out other than to the grocery store or something similar in nearly a year. This night was huge for me.

Sam and George both gave me their mother hen smiles. The smile where they are conveying they are so proud of you, but we can leave at any time because deep down, we know you are fragile and break easily. Screw them. They didn't know new Frankie was kicking old, scared, NOT FUNNY Frankie to the curb. Tonight, I was out to prove to my friends and myself, that new Frankie was kick ass.

We flagged down a server, but all we got was a whole lot of staring from one waitress and scowling from another. But then, the George and Sam factor meant she was drawn like a moth to the mother lovin' flame. George, being married to 2014's sexiest man around, Finn Lowry, had women asking her for Finn's autograph all the time. I didn't know how she handled it with such grace. If that was me, each time some woman asked for my husband's deets, while I was obviously pregnant, I would have practiced my karate moves, on their fake boobs just to sit back and watch them burst.

Then there's Sam. Sam drew people to her like she was sunshine and they had been living in the dark for a near eternity. There was a reason she was a super successful movie star. We all met one fateful night at a producer's party in the Hollywood hills. Sam was the star of the movie, I was friends with the art director and the movie was an adaptation of one of George's best sellers. We bonded over mojitos and misery. George and I are natural introverts, gravitating towards each other outside, on the balcony in the relative peace of a secluded corner. I found her there while I was attempting to ignore my fiancé, who had insisted I bring him, so he could, once again, be the centre of attention.

So, I was hiding from him on the balcony and sat down next to George. It was after I had listened to five solid minutes of crickets chirping, that I became uncomfortable with the silence coming from her. The feeling was mutual, as we both turned to each other and started talking at the same time.

While we were bonding over our hatred for everything LA, Sam barged in, dove behind the cabana cover we were sitting in and told us to carry on as if she wasn't there. And us being us, we did. Eventually, she began to contribute to our conversation and we haven't looked back since. She's our trio's glue. Sam pushes us two recluses out into the real world when we need a good shove, but covers us in her protective glow when she knows we need shelter. She's the main reason George found the courage to let Finn in and she's one half of the reason I am whole today. The other half is sitting across the table openly staring at the goings on filing it all away somewhere in that wild imagination of hers.

The servers were still alternating between giving us the stink eye and openly staring and it was starting to really freak me out.

George leaned in and whispered, "Does anyone feel like something really odd is happening here? Why did this place go all freaky silent and why did that waitress look like she was trying to voodoo us out of here?"

"Agreed. Franks, what have you been up to around here? Some weird fucking mojo shit is going down with the females and-" Sam abruptly broke off what she was about to say and got a glassed over look in her eyes. "Never mind. I think I might move here actually. Oh and there's our answer. It's a tall, hot vision in navy walking over here that's got these ladies all riled up and he brought some friends."

"What are you talking about Sam?"

She hopped up and scooted her chair away from me and grabbed a chair from behind her. "Hardy! And friends. Join us."

The chair beside me was instantly occupied. Oh jeez. Hardy in his uniform. What girl didn't go a little bit gaga over a man in uniform. Add to that, the man inside this uniform was tall, dark, muscled and I would expect built perfectly in every way, then I wasn't at all surprised my heart rate sped up and my insides slowed down. He was lovely to stare at in every way, but it was his eyes that had done me in and won me over. Deep, dark brown with flecks of amber that offered a version of life that I had never thought possible.

He leaned over and whispered in my ear. "Hey, Red. Come here often?"

I smirked and raised my left eyebrow. "You're here."

"Just finished my shift and could use a beer. You got a problem with that?" He gave me his own version of an eyebrow lift that made him look like a crazed serial killer. I burst out laughing and instantly covered my mouth with my hand. "Shit, babe. Did you just laugh?"

I looked around the table and saw George and Sam smiling at me with eyes as round as saucers. "You're still not funny."

We locked eyes and just grinned like idiots at each other until I noticed the uncomfortable silence surrounding us. Never one to let silence go wasted, Sam cleared her throat and nudged Hardy. "Hey Romeo, are you gonna introduce your posse or are you two just going to sit there making moony eyes at each other all night?"

"Ladies, this is Josh and Will. Guys, this here beauty is Sam and beside her is George and this one here," he slung an arm around me, trailing his fingers across my neck, "this is Frankie."

"All clear to me now, Chief," said Will. He turned to Sam and started up a conversation, George was texting, most likely Finn, so Josh turned to me and asked if we had ordered yet.

"Well, we haven't had the warmest welcome here," I said. "It went pretty silent when we walked in and for some weird reason, our waitress seems to have a super hate on for us."

Josh snickered. "Doesn't surprise me. That's Lindsay. She'll get a hate on for anyone who thinks to steal her Hardy boy away."

"Josh," Hardy snapped.

"What? Why would she think I'm stealing him away?" I turned to face Hardy. "Are you two together?"

"Not in this lifetime. Except, I could kiss you for choosing this bar on this night, sitting in this section, 'cause you're doing me a hell of a favour showing her there is no us."

I let out a long, frustrated breath. I remembered seeing Lindsay at the BBQ and she must have been the leader of the pack of she-wolves that wanted to hump Hardy's leg. So, in the past twenty four hours, I had been jealous, excited, elated, embarrassed, despondent and horny. The last having just arrived about ten minutes ago. Lucky, lucky me. I went from feeling nothing other than fear all day, every day to all these emotions in the past few weeks, and to top it off, now it looked like I was into Hardy. Like, bad enough that I was about to do something I hadn't done since college.

I got up from my seat, looked Hardy in the eyes and turned on my heel and headed for the bar where Lindsay was holding court with her pack of minions. They stared at me with looks of pure venom, but little did they know, I had looked into the eyes of real, true evil and lived to tell the tale, and this here show of theirs was child's play.

When they finally figured out I was headed straight into enemy territory, they had the good sense their momma gave them to start to look suspicious of my intentions. I didn't have to turn around to know my girls had my back, but I was a bit nervous as to what Hardy would think about me when I was done whatever the hell it was I was going to do.

I stopped in front of Lindsay and smiled my bestest, friendliest smile ever and she totally took the bait.

"Can I help you?" Her voice grated on me and the false sweetness of it was like pouring gasoline on my low burning fire.

"Yes, yes you sure can. My friends and I walked in here over twenty minutes ago and we haven't had a server over to our table so we can order our drinks."

"Oh, well, you see, you're sitting in a section that isn't in a service area."

Oh, it was so on honey. "Really? So, the other tables all around us are but we aren't? Huh, that's really strange." I was still speaking to her as if I was a general dolt and had no clue she was attempting to pull one over on me. "Ok, so I guess we'll just move to a different table so we can get service."

"Well, actually, most of the tables aren't being served tonight. See, we're a little short staffed. You're going to have to walk to the bar like the rest of our customers to get your own beer." She smiled, like she had won some sort of contest with me.

"Ok, sure, that sounds fine. That works out better anyway. Then I can stay at a table that fits all of us in real close." I leaned in close and lowered my voice. "I'm really happy about that. I'm here on my first date with that super-hot fireman over there." I paused and turned back towards Hardy and did a little smile and a wave. He waved back without giving anything away on his face. He was letting me play this one out and I was thankful for that.

"Isn't he hot? Ugh, I'm so lucky he finally got up the nerve to ask me out today. We've been hanging out every day for the past three weeks and I was wondering when we might get to progressing past the just touching point." I winked conspiratorially at her. "It's good I get to stay at that table and get squeezed in close with him. I love the heat his body gives off. So warm and delicious. My friends, Sam and George will be happy too. George being pregnant and all. Imagine, being married to 2014's hottest man alive! And of course, Sam, is always the diva. A-list actresses don't like to be moved around or pissed off. Their temper is always just simmering below the surface and they love to throw bad press around to establishments they encounter that they are inconvenienced in."

I decided to finish up and get my drink so I could go back to enjoying my first night out in forever. "So, let me sum it all up for you. I am a patron of this establishment, along with my friends and date. We are all thirsty and plan on being here the entire night, and would like to get on with our plan to drink and dance. If you don't get a server over to that table pronto, not only will Hardy and his friends take us somewhere else, but I'm going to let my best friend Sam call up her best friend Finn and together, they can call some of their favourite PR people to make sure this bar and it's servers, never get a crowd of people to serve ever again." I paused and took a deep breath. "Are we good?"

God, that was bitchy. Where in the hell did that come from? I turned and strode back to our table and without looking at anyone, sat the hell back down and re-evaluated my life in five seconds. I wasn't normally mean and bitchy but something in me had changed. I think it was called a back bone, or a bitch bone.

Sam, of course, was the first to say something. "Franks, can we come up with a bat signal in the sky for the next time I need to put a skanky hoe bag in her place? No matter where I am?"

George was up next. "Yeah, Finn should have you on speed dial for me. That kind of shit happens to me all the time. But what I want to know, is where in the ever loving hell did you just pull that out of? You are our peace keeper Franks. Now you're our war chief!"

My face was red and I had no idea what Hardy and his friends must be thinking. I finally had the courage to lift my head up and see if they were considering heading out to another bar where the girls inside weren't raving bitches.

I felt a finger poke me in the side and turned to look at Hardy. He had his one eyebrow lifted, scowl face on again and I wasn't sure if that was good or bad. I didn't have time to find out, as our server, Lindsay, had chosen to finally come and take our drink orders. And I guess she had decided to give me the finger, as she sidled up in between Hardy and Josh and proceeded to take their orders.

I gave up and hung my head in defeat. I couldn't compete with her assets. Literally. And those assets where on full display. My much smaller, much less fake assets were no match for these. I propped my head in my hand and just waited for it to be my turn. Except my turn never came. When she skipped me and went to Hardy, he ordered for the both of us.

"Frankie will have a mojito, Lindsay and I'll just take a beer." He reached under the table and started a search and rescue project on my leg. He finally found what he was looking for and grabbed a hold of my hand and laced our fingers together. A tingle started climbing around my arms and I had no idea what in the hell was going on. I didn't hold hands. Period.

The bitch just kept right on digging herself a hole. "Now Hardy, you know we don't have any of those fancy drinks here. We're just a down home, local establishment, serving up go old American drinks." She leaned a little closer to him to emphasize her all American assets.

Hardy, bless his heart, wasn't buying any today. "Ok, then she'll have a beer, with a side of limes, please Lindsay." He then dragged our joined hands up on top of the table, smiled at her and effectively dismissed her when he leaned over and whispered in my ear, "That was awesome babe. You and I need to hang out in public more often." He softly kissed the spot in front of my ear where no one could see and sat back. His thumb was gently drawing circles on my hand. Back and forth figure eights. I stared at our joined hands, mesmerized by the motion of his thumb and thrilled at the small shock waves it was sending up and down my body. Who knew a thumb touch could feel so good? Who also knew I would ever be able to feel this after my self-imposed isolation?

I looked up and could see Lindsay still standing there, trying to figure out her next move. She must have decided on a temporary retreat, as she turned on her heel and left to get our drinks. Next came the uncomfortable silence, which for my friends, was weird. I looked up to see why Sam at the very least wasn't saying anything and caught her wiping a stray tear from her eye. I looked across to George to see her a big hormonal mess with tears leaking like a river down her face.

I didn't want them to make a scene and I especially didn't want them to have to explain to Hardy and his friends the reason for their tears, so I dropped our hands back out of sight, untangled my hand from his and turned to give him a small smile. He looked back at me with a furrowed brow. That was me. Two steps forward, one step back. I think I had pushed myself as far as I could tonight, but it appeared Hardy didn't think so. He stood up and grabbed my hand on his way by. He leaned down and whispered in my ear, "a minute of your time, Red? Please?"

He really didn't give me any choice, as he refused to let go of my hand as he continued in a forward motion towards the bathrooms. Just when I thought I was about to get invited to a secret meeting in the urinals, he veered right into an alcove that looked like it used to house a pay phone.

Before I knew what the hell was happening, he catapulted me backwards, swung his free arm behind me and positioned me against the wall with his back to the bar. "Ok, Frankie. You and I need to have a chat. I do not in the holy hell understand what has got into you in the past few days, but I am not going to complain about it one bit."

He was close. Too close and I was about to lose it. He must have sensed something was wrong as he slowly, like he was dealing with a wild, frightened animal, lifted his hands until they were framing my face. Gently, he eased his fingers into my scalp and began to lightly massage around my ears, effectively calming me down. A bit. I still was miles away from accepting aggressive touch from a man. Hardy didn't know what kind of fire he was playing with.

"That's it, baby," he whispered. "Relax. I'm not going to hurt you." His voice cracked and I nearly lost my battle to keep him at bay when I saw the anguish in his eyes. "Who did this to you, Red? Who took the fire away from my girl?"

Oh shit, he did not just call me his girl. As if my entire body had decided to follow my traitorous heart, a single tear made its escape. It's path clear and focused, straight and quick down my left cheek to splash over his massive thumb. "Don't. Please, Hardy. Don't." My voice was barely above a whisper. I could not let this out here and now. I owed him my story, but not here. Not in the dark alcove in this shit hole of a bar.

Slowly, I raised my own hands to find his and held on, willing that tear to be the lone escapee. "Not here, please. Not tonight. When the girls leave you and I need to sit down and talk. You deserve to know it all Hardy, but I'm warning you. It's not pretty. It's not a happy ending and for us, I'm not able to give you that either."

"Baby, do you think I haven't figured that out yet? I know you've got secrets and I can tell you're afraid. I am too. We're two peas in this fucked up pod. You're right. Here isn't the place to get into our ugly pasts. But before I let you go back to kick some more of Lindsay's ass, I need you to know something."

"What?"

"I've spent these past few weeks getting to know you. And yes, before you interrupt as you are fixin' to do, I am aware you and I have had some pretty amazing one sided conversations, but still. I felt it. So, what I need you to know, before you walk back out there and convince yourself this isn't going to work, I need you to know that I am into you. So into you, I can't do anything but work. 'Cause at work, I can get my mind off you. What you're doing when we're not running, what you're painting, why you moved here, when would you notice I'm into you. That shit. All day. Then it leads to me planning all the things I am going to do to that crazy body of yours. And then I'm headed right back to work, wishing for a damn fire to ignite and consume me 'cause that's got to hurt less than my dick all day long."

He leaned in close enough that our noses were side by side and did this small, intimate nose rub, that I if I thought about it too long, would feel like being scented, but it was oddly sensual. His hands had left my face and were straight up in the air, palms flat to the wall behind me and I silently thanked him for using his hands to keep his body from caging me in. He instinctively knew touching was my issue.

He pushed away from the wall, grabbed my hand in his and pulled us back out of our cocoon and into the real world. I revelled in the feel of his hand in mine, of his thumb once again rubbing my hand into a state of erotic wonder and the newfound friendship that we had all found tonight. I wasn't going to let anyone take that accomplishment away from me.

He sat me down beside him and possessively placed his hand on my thigh and pulled it so it was touching his own. Then he moved his other hand to slip around my waist and began to play with my t-shirt. He lifted it up and began to lightly stroke my sensitive skin. He lit me on fire. My brain had been put to sleep by his magic fingers and my heart and vagina were coming out to play. They were excited. They hadn't been allowed out after dark in a very long time.

We stayed for a couple more drinks, before I noticed George fighting falling face first onto the table. "George, let's go home."

"No, I'm fine Franks. Just a little tired."

"You're not just tired, George. You're pregnant. I've been there before, I-" Oh shit. He didn't know I'd been there before. Damn it, why did I have to always speak before I thought things through? I have worked really hard to keep Hardy separate from my past and now I just gave away one of my hugest secrets.

He grabbed my hand again under the table and gave it a squeeze and then began his patented calming technique of thumb circles. I hoped he was conveying his wish for me to relax and not worry about what I revealed, but I was so messed up, I had no idea what was going on in his mind. One thing was clear, he and I needed to talk and set the records straight. He needed to know there was no future with me. I was on the move more than I wasn't and this location had almost hit it's expiry point. I could feel the anxiety building. I would never feel safe in one location for too long. The problem was, I was beginning to feel safe here. False senses of security were harmful to my health. I needed a next step plan and I needed to ensure Hardy was on board.

I decided packing it in may be our best option and it would keep me out of trouble a little longer. "Look, let's just hang out at my place and have a girl's night in."

Hardy piped up at that statement. "Girls night? What about the rest of us?"

"Sorry pal," Sam butt in. "Vaginas only."

The other two guys at the table snorted into their beers like immature high school students, but Hardy looks genuinely upset and hurt. I grab his hand and lace my fingers with his. "Hey, I need a night with my friends, O.K? They live across the country and we rarely get to have this time and there are a few things that we need to clear up. Can our talk wait until they leave on Sunday?"

"Two whole nights? I'll miss you babe, but I have to work anyway. Besides, I'll see you tomorrow for our group run anyway, right?" He winks at George, who snorts oh so ladylike and points at Sam and I. "Enjoy that ladies. Nothing better than running on the beach while hung over. Nope, nothing better."

I threw a wet napkin at her and get up to leave. We all throw in some money and make our way to the door. Hardy grabs my hand on the way out, effectively shutting up Lindsay and her super scary gang. I haven't been a jealous bitch since my bestie stole my boyfriend and played spin the bottle with him in fifth grade, but it's back with a vengeance and I hate it. Jealousy is such a wasted emotion.

Hardy squeezes my hand and brings me back to present day and my current problems. We stopped at my car and he turns me to face him. "Frankie, we need to talk."

"Yeah, we really do, but not tonight. Tonight, I just need some time with the girls." He looks like he wants to say something but changes his mind. Instead, he brushes my run away hair off my face and tucks it behind my ear. It's his turn to be lost inside his mind now. He is looking at me but with eyes that aren't seeing me. It reminds me this guy has secrets he's keeping too. We really do need to talk.

He blinks and snaps out of it when Sam and George honk the horn to get us moving. "See you tomorrow?"

I groan. I plan on getting completely shitfaced intoxicated tonight for the first time in years and there is no way in hell I can even consider running on a beach tomorrow. "Do we have to? I don't really think I'm going to be up for it."

Just then, his pager goes off, along with Josh and Will's in a chorus of urgency. Hardy leans in to give me a quick brush on the cheek and turns to go back to work. As he jogs away, he shouts out to the night, "tomorrow, Red. I expect you and Sam on the beach in hot running gear. Running."

Even though he has reached Josh's truck and probably can't hear me, I scream back, "not happening, Hardy Hanson." He turns his head towards me as he hops up into the truck and graces me with one of his huge grins, dimples and all and just laughs and then takes off into the night to save women and children from burning buildings. Just another day at the office for my guy. Yup, I said it. My guy.

Chapter 13

Frankie

I'm drooling. My face is disgustingly wet. What the hell? I'm frozen, uncomfortable and have a hangover to rival the mother of all hangovers. And again, my face is wet. And salty. Ew.

I try to burrow down into the nest I have made for myself but realize this is a futile effort. I have no nest to speak of. No covers, no flat surface. It feels suspiciously like I am asleep on one of my deck chairs. Outside. Hmm. It was then I heard the sniffle. The sniffle that sounded oddly like a snicker. God, if only it didn't feel like my eyelashes were glued to my eyelids I might consider opening them up. I also had a feeling that the sun beating down on me would give me an instant ice pick headache. More wetness hit my face and that ended my argument with myself. I pried one eye open to see what in the hell was going on.

The light was blinding, the pain, the agony but the vision was purely angelic. Dark mop of curls flying every which way, straight nose, deep brown eyes and a mouth that was currently twitching all over trying not to release the laughter that laid beneath.

"Hardy," I croaked out. "What the fuck are you doing here?"

"Such a sweet girl." He smiled and raised an eyebrow. "It's well past ten o'clock Red. I believe we had a jogging date and I am here to find out why you didn't show," he paused. "Again. I'm beginning to think that you don't really like jogging with me, or maybe it's just me. Or then again, it could have something to do with the fact that you were sleeping outside in a chair without a blanket or much on in the way of clothes."

He raked his eyes pointedly down my body and I cursed my inability to hold my alcohol. Sam, damn her. She was responsible for this. The problem was, I couldn't fathom moving for all the blankets and clothes on the eastern seaboard.

"Hit the bottle a little hard last night, Frankie?"

"Ow, Hardy, please make the world stop spinning and while you're at it, make this blazing sun go away too. Oh, and grab me a blanket so you'll stop staring at me like a perv."

"I'll never stop staring at you, babe, but I'll take pity on you and get you a blanket."

He turned and grabbed a throw that Sam or I must have left on the deck as we stumbled around last night. I vaguely remember telling her I was going to star gaze and contemplate the mystical workings of the universe prior to heading to bed. I must have passed out as soon as I sat down. He tucked the blanket gently around me, lifted my legs and scooted himself underneath me and rested my legs back down on his lap. He picked up a foot and started to massage it and I sighed in ecstasy.

"So," he began. "What are you ladies up to today?"

"Zero, nada, zilch. You?"

"Working."

"You sure work a lot, Hardy"

He picked up my sunglasses from the side table and slipped them on my face. "Yeah, I do. Keeps me busy."

"What else keeps you busy?"

He picked up my other foot and began to work on it. "Not much. Work, running and not much else. I try to keep my time free in case of an emergency."

It was getting hard to formulate complete sentences with the massages and my pounding head. "You don't do anything else?"

He stopped his massage and moved my legs so he could get up. As he walked towards my door, he mumbled, "no." Then he disappeared into my house and instead of wondering what the hell he was up to, I just closed my eyes and tried out some new force of will relaxation techniques. Before I could get very far, he was back. And he came bearing gifts. He held a large glass of water and my giant bottle of Advil. The man was simply amazing.

He set the glass down beside me and opened the bottle. "Open up." I obediently opened my mouth and he popped in two Advil, followed by a drink of water.

"Thanks."

He pulled up a chair and plopped down next to me. "Ok, so, I'm gonna get going. Do you need me to get you anything else?"

I looked into those deep brown eyes and didn't know what the hell to do. Yes, I needed a lot of things, topping the list, him. But I couldn't let myself go there. I was getting close to moving time again and he was just too damn adorable. He clearly got attached to a project. Figures he would decide on me as his current project. He was the kind of man who needed a woman to give him her heart and soul and I knew that couldn't be me. I couldn't stay in one place too long. He might find me.

"No, thanks."

He held my gaze, hands on his hips, looking like he needed to say something. No way in hell was I going to let him say whatever it was. I half turned and snuggled down deep into the blanket he had covered me with and closed my eyes. It was then he got me again.

I felt him tuck one of my usual stray hairs, softly behind my ear and trail his finger down my face and neck. He then grabbed the edge of my blanket and tugged it up so I was completely covered and protected. 'Cause I was getting the feeling that's what he did best. Protect people.

A mere moment later he sealed the deal with a feather light brush of his lips on mine and a whispered goodbye. I heard the stairs creek his exit and silently wondered what the hell I was going to do. Resisting this man seemed like a super power I needed to acquire. Stat.

The girls and I spent the rest of the day dozing and talking and assuring George's husband, Finn, that George and the baby were perfectly fine and that they would be boarding their flight on time at the crack of dawn the next day. Although I gave George a hard time about Finn being so attached to her and constantly worried about her wellbeing, it didn't hold any weight. I was insanely jealous of their relationship. I had no idea if that amount of adoration would ever find its way to me in a partner, but I hoped that one day, I could stop being afraid and stay in the stillness of life to uncover even a tiny portion of that amount of love.

We were finishing up dinner on the deck and sipping our wine when they went on the attack. Frankly, I was wondering what had taken them so long. I had almost made it out of Dodge without the usual uncomfortable check-in from my two best friends.

Sam dove in first. "Franks, any sign of him?"
I heaved a deep sigh. I guess I might as well get it over with and then I could come up with a strategy to shift the focus to Sam's absolute shit-show of a love life. "No, no sign. But I feel like it's nearly time. I'm going to start researching my next stop."

George sat back rubbing her belly. "Why? Why can't you just settle in? This Hardy guy seems like he could be an interesting incentive to stick around a bit longer than your usual few months?"

"I can't George. You know that. I'm good at running, not staying."
"You know that asshole has been slowly edging his way back into the circles of influence again. I've seen him at a few parties I've been at lately." Sam took a giant gulp of her water. "He's up to something. He's been trying to get friendly with me the last two times I've seen him. I'm pretty sure he's scared I might nutball him right in front of his fancy friends."

"Why didn't you tell me he was trying to talk to you?"

"I didn't want to worry you unnecessarily, Franks. Look at you. You're panicking and I just told you two minutes ago. You're already running through all the things you need to do to get ready to run."
I stared out into the water. She was right. I was going to have to learn to deal with news of his life in ways other than exit strategies. He lived a very public life. High powered politicians didn't just stay home and rent movies on a Saturday night. Especially those that lived in LA. They stayed visible in their circles that included the wealthy and the famous.

"Please keep me in the loop. I want to know where he is and what he wants with you. Please, it's just who I am. I can't let myself forget why I'm hiding out here. Getting too comfortable means getting dead."

"Sorry Franks. Of course I will. Let's talk about something else. For example, Hardy. Yes, let's talk about Fireman Hardy. What is in the hell is going on with you two?"

"There is no us two, Sam. We're friends."

George decided to speak up, but it came out more as a bark. "Frankie, it's us. And there is definitely and you and him. I think he says so, so that means it's so."

"Is that baby working on sucking out your last few remaining brain cells?"

She didn't reply. Just stuck out her tongue at me. "Mature, George. So, mature."

"Out with it Franks." Sam wasn't going to let me stall any longer. "We've got an early flight and the baby factory here has to get to bed before her alarm goes off and Finn, the pregnant wife whisperer, calls me to make sure she's tucked into bed, dreaming of sugar plums and his dick."

I spit out the water I had gulped. "Oh my God, Sam. That's awesome."

"Awesome and true. He programmed her phone to remind her to go to bed and get enough rest, and then he texts me to make sure she's following the rules. And please, her hormones are off the chart crazy making her hornier than a mountain goat."

"Excuse me," George, looking indignant cut in. "I am capable of speaking and thinking for myself. For starters, Finn is driving me nuts with his cranky pants, alpha male demands and secondly, his dick is something to dream about so fuck you."

Sam turned to me. "Well, do you dream of plums and Hardy dicks?"

"Jesus, Sam. So none of your business."

She nodded her head. "You do. I can see it in your eyes."

"I don't! Shut it!" I puffed up my chest and got as high and mighty as I could. Then lost it all when I looked at their faces and fell over laughing. "Ok, well, I might have thought about it. Just a tiny wee bit." I held up my fingers to emphasize my point and burst out laughing again. "Well, let's hope it's not a tiny wee bit, but you know what I mean."

We fell over in a ridiculous fit of teenaged giggles. We laughed harder than I have laughed in ages. See Hardy, I thought to myself. I'm funny. We laughed that stupid laugh that you couldn't stop with best friends, 'cause every time you looked at each other, you burst out laughing again, until you fell over, clutching your out of shape stomach and begging the others to stop. Or your best friend is five months pregnant and pees herself. Whatever comes first.

"Ew, George," Sam said. "What the hell?"

By this time, George's laugh had actually morphed into a cry. A loud, obnoxious, we might get a few animals looking to mate with her kind of cry. Through her tears, she was trying to speak but it was all coming out Greek.

"George," I said. "Get a grip. What are you trying to say?"

She took a few half breaths, sobbed and slowly got herself under control, that is, until the hiccups came. Then we collapsed back into a fit of giggles and we were helpless to try to stop them.

Finally, George got herself nearly all the way under control and threw her head down on the table. "I just peed my pants. And it wasn't the first time. What the hell, guys? Why does procreating have to be so messy? You wouldn't believe the other shit that comes out of me."

Sam jumped in. "No, no, you're probably right Georgie. So, just keep it to yourself. It's not the kind of information I can't live without." She got up, came around the side of George's chair and lifted her up and out of it. "Come on, let's get you into a fresh pair of jammies and clean undies and tucked into bed before that hulk of a husband finds out I haven't been following his instructions then I won't be allowed to be alone with you and the baby."

I scooted around to George's other side and together we laughed and dragged her into her room, got her undressed and pushed her into the shower. She didn't stop weeping, hiccupping or laughing much through the whole process, so it took some time. Time in which Finn texted and called Sam and I to make sure we were taking care of her. Even though I rolled my eyes and complained about him, I did wonder what it would be like to be so cherished. So cared for. So loved.

An hour later, Sam and I said our goodnights and I fell into a fitful sleep. My girls were going home the next day. I was going to have to head back to reality and figure out what my next steps were. And then there was Hardy. He and I needed to talk. It was time to tell him as much as I could, but still tell him nothing at all. He most likely wasn't going to like it, but it didn't matter. I needed to leave and the less Hardy liked me, the better.

I don't know who I thought I was fooling with that statement, but I was sticking with it. I fell asleep with a smile on my face thinking about him. Maybe just a kiss. Just one small thing to take with me when I left.

Chapter 14

Frankie

I waved goodbye to the girls and wiped a tear or two off my cheeks and went back inside to try to convince myself that a run was a good idea. I was sure going to miss those girls. The next time I moved, neither would be around to help me. George wouldn't want to leave LA again being pregnant and Sam was heading to Ireland for a few months soon to film her next movie. My next move would have to be a simple one. The bags I had and that was all. Without any help, it couldn't be more difficult than that.

I tidied up the kitchen and checked the time. I had twenty minutes to go until I met him at the turn around point. Better get moving.

I headed out the back door, locked up and readied myself to go. As I was stretching, I noticed a few people out on the beach. It seemed early for this many people to be out. I slowly glanced around landed on a man walking back from the shore. He looked familiar but I couldn't place him. The man disappeared over the sand dunes and I tried my best to clear him from my thoughts. I didn't have much success. I was becoming paranoid. It was really time to go. If he had tracked me down, I knew I didn't stand a chance at surviving. He would end me out here, where no one knew of our connection.

I focused in on my breathing and pushed him from my mind. If I was going to survive this run today, I needed to focus. I was exhausted and emotional and adding paranoid to my list wasn't going to do me any favours.

I took off down the beach. After a bit, I fell into my running trance and before I knew it, I could see him waiting for me up ahead. My heart rate increased, if that was even possible, and I began to get nervous. I could hear my breathing coming out in huffs, and my leg muscles began to cramp. I needed water. And a lobotomy. Maybe not in that order.

He smiled his crazy mega smile, tucked his IPod away and fell in behind me just as we had been doing for the past few weeks. Today though, I wasn't having it. For starters, there was a little more jiggle in my wiggle this week as I had taken a few days off exercising. Add to that, I had run out of thongs to wear today and my spandexed rear end had a bad case of granny pantyitous. But most importantly, I needed to take control. And even though, one might think he was the follower and didn't have control, he did. I was ready to direct this relationship where I wanted it to go. Where in the hell that was, I was going to make it up as I went along, but still, I had to start somewhere.

I slowed my pace and shifted towards the loose sand, instantly regretting my decision. Suddenly, keeping alongside him became a feat I was nowhere near able to accomplish. My legs began to burn, my heart rate could possibly have jumped into the danger zone, and now Hardy was looking at me, not only wearing granny panties, but with sweat stinging my eyes and my mouth open and gasping for air like a land locked fish. Shit, my plan had already started out destined for failure.

He slowed his pace to a crawl and turned towards me. "What are you doing?"

"Jogging."

"No, no you're not. You're wheezing, that's for sure, but I don't think what you are doing can be called jogging. I don't think arms and legs are supposed to flail like that when you're running."

I gave him my best attempt at an indignant look, but I'm sure it came off looking more like that same open mouthed fish look from before. "Judge not, lest ye be judged, or something like that."

"Now you're trying to quote scripture. Huh. What are you up to?"

"I'm not up to anything. I just thought maybe I would run beside you today instead of in front."

He just looked at me, shrugged and kept going. We finally made it to our turn around point, and for the first time, I begged for a break. We turned back towards my house and took it at a walking pace while I drank some water and attempted to catch my breath.

I tried to talk, but nothing would come out. We weren't sharing a comfortable silence. We were sharing an excruciatingly painful silence. One of us had to speak soon, or I would and I still wasn't done formulating my plan.

By the time I had finally stopped wheezing and the stinging sweat had begun to coagulate, we had returned almost all the way back to my house. So much for a run. Halfway just wasn't going to cut it.

We collapsed onto my deck stairs and just stared at the waves coming in off the ocean.

"So-"

"So?"

And then we both burst out laughing. "God," I said. "I feel like a teenager talking to a boy I like for the first time."

He turned to look at me and the breeze caught a pile of his sticky, curled hair. "You like me?"

I rolled my eyes. "I think that's pretty evident"

"No, no, it really isn't. You're pretty damn hard to read, Red. At the exact moment I think I know which way is up, you tell me definitively, it's down."
"Do I? I'm sorry. I have issues. Well, my issues have issues, I have so many issues."

"Yep, I'm on the way back down again."

I nudged him with my shoulder. "Ok, here's how it gonna go. I need to shower, and I'm pretty sure you do too." I laughed. "No, don't try to deny it. It's true. So, we shower. And before you say it, no, not together. We reconvene back here after and talk."

"Deal, but I still think I don't need a shower."

"You do, so go. I won't let you in my house smelling like that."

"Fine, I'm going. But I'll be back, Frankie." He leaned in really, really close. So close, I could feel his breath and smell his sweat. "You aren't hiding from me anymore." He reached up to clasp my chin in his two fingers. "I'm coming back and you're showing me all your cards. No more secrets between us. Got it?"

I blinked, then silently cursed myself. That was the sign of the liar when you were playing poker. Damn. "Got it. The truth and nothing but."

He still had a hold of my chin as he rose to go so I had no choice but to rise with him. He leaned back in and it looked like he was going to kiss me. But no, he had other ideas. He closed our distance to slices of air until all I could feel was his hot breath exchanging itself with mine. Oh, he was good. He wasn't going to kiss me, he was going to make me beg for it. Bastard. What he didn't know was that stubborn was my secret middle name. Even after knowing what was best for me, I still wouldn't give it to him. It was game on. Besides, I still had to rehearse my "this is me being honest" speech while showering. I had things to do and he had better let me go so I could get to them.

"See you in a few, Red," he whispered softly against my ear, effectively shutting down all second thoughts I was about to embark on.

I lost my cool then. I didn't say anything snappy, no catch ya laters, just a good old fashioned oglc. And it was awesome.

As I turned to go inside and shower, I caught sight of the stranger, back on the beach, but this time, dressed in a swimsuit and hat. He had his back to me, but I sensed I knew him somehow. As I watched, Hardy jogged past him and he waved in greeting and I decided to let it go and focused on one foot in front of the other. There was no way I was going to answer the door in a towel or not totally ready for the day. I had no idea what in the world was going to happen, but I had better at least make an effort in case something did. I needed shave off the cavewoman hair in all the wrong places, pronto.

Chapter 15

Hardy

My leg was bouncing up a storm in the cab of my truck as I drove home. I hadn't been this nervous about seeing a girl in a long, long time. Something was different here. Frankie was bringing out things in me that hadn't seen much or any action since Sarah.

I was terrified I was going to fuck this up. It was what guys do, after all. We fuck shit up. Especially relationships. I had to get a hold of myself and my errant, bouncing leg.

I pulled into my drive and practically ran out of the truck and into my house. Chuck was dancing circles around me, but I didn't have a whole lot of time for him today. I quickly let him out and watched him choose the perfect patch to roll around in. He was such a nut. He came back in and I ran down the hall to get ready. I was such a girl when it came to getting ready. I had to shower, then do my hair, then add cologne. Then it was finding the right outfit. I needed it to say, I cared, but casually. The casual care.

I ended up taking a couple of hours to get ready. She was probably going to kill me or laugh at me. I said goodbye to Chuck, sent a text to the neighbourhood teen who walked him when I couldn't. She took him over to her house for sleepovers all the time and he was spoiled rotten there. I hopped back in the truck and started the twenty minute drive back to her place. My leg started up its anxiety dance again and all it did was set me on edge.

This woman meant something to me and that was a huge step in a new direction. I hadn't handled these feelings yet and I wasn't sure I was going to do anything right tonight. Frankie practically had a handle with care sign stamped on her head and I had my own issues. I needed to set that all aside and just let it happen, but that was easier said than done. We needed to get a few things out in the open and today was the day. I wasn't going to share much. Today was her day to finally give me the answers I was waiting for.

Chapter 16

Frankie

I was pacing. What the hell was wrong with me? I don't pace. He was taking forever to get back. It was getting on mid-afternoon and he still hadn't made it back. Well, I guess if I was going to pace, I might as well pace myself over to my empty canvas. I picked up a paint brush and began to let my anxiety out through the delicate brush strokes. Soon, the strokes became more aggressive, then cooled, than curved. I became completely lost and exhilarated in my work.

Then, straight out of a what not to do when in a horror movie situation, I screamed at the top of my lungs and turned, as a hand shot out and grabbed a hold of my waist. As I was turning, I took my brush with me and instantly decided to use it as a weapon against my attacker. Except all it did was paint a beautiful shade of blue straight across Hardy's face. Holy shit. This was just so not good.

"Hardy! Oh God, I'm so sorry." I grabbed the hem of my shirt and attempted to wipe him off, but only succeeded in smearing it in more. "I'm so sorry. Shit, so sorry."

He grabbed my wrists and held them at bay before I could inflict anymore damage, since I had still yet to drop the paint brush. "Frankie, relax."

I couldn't tell if he was enraged or, wait, no, he was enraged. And so I did what I always do in uncomfortable situations, laugh. Except, once again, in front of Hardy, I'm laughing and snorting and wait for it, yup, now I'm crying all in the span of less than a minute. So, so attractive and already this plan has gone completely off the rails.

However, there is an upside. His face has gone from enraged, to pained. "I so want to be mad at you right now, but I just can't. In fact, that most attractive laughter you're letting out, is catching."

I was completely immobilized by my unladylike laughing. So immobilized that in the blink of an eye, he grabbed my paint brush and swiped right then left across my nose. He finished his masterpiece with a dot on the end of my nose. I froze. I was stone cold sober and now I was the enraged one. "Oh no, you so did not do that! Hardy, it was an accident. I can't believe you're being so childish."

He smiled his stupid dimpled smile that surely had woman dropping their panties to do his bidding all over town, but not this girl. He was going to pay for that.

I dashed around him and grabbed the first brush I could and whipped around to attack him with the red paint, but damn the man. He was too fast and had anticipated my moves. He easily captured my wrists and once again, I was his captive.

"Red, no more. Unless of course, you have some edible paint? Now, that's an art project I could get behind."

"Perv." I huffed out a defeated breath and nearly stomped my foot. I hated losing, which brought my playful thoughts to a grinding halt. I needed to get us back on track or I was never going to get to the points I needed to make so I could see where this was going.

"Truce."

He raised a gloriously handsome eyebrow. "Truce? What is this? War?"

"No, just, I mean it. I'm truly sorry and I deserved that retaliation. Can we just leave it at that, clean up and talk?"

He eyed me warily. "How do I know I can trust you?"

"You don't."

He kept looking at me, as if he could see past all my lies and walls and excuses into his own version of who I was. He was assessing his ability to trust me. I would too. I had failed a whole lot of people, some of the most important people in the whole wide world to me, just to protect that son of a bitch's secret.

Slowly, I felt the pressure release from my wrists. At the same time, he began to lower his arms until our paint brushes were out of the lines of fire. He released me completely, but didn't step back from where we were toe to toe. I glanced down and the spell was broken.

"Where's your bathroom?"

I pointed with the offending brush, careful not to break the tenuous truce we had. "Down the hall, first door on your right."

He smiled and headed that way. I put the brushes away and hurried after him. I grabbed an old washcloth in the back of my linen closet so he didn't permanently discolour my matching sets. "Here, can you please use this one to clean up?"

He took it with a funny look on his face, like he was here, but his mind was somewhere else. His face was frozen in a half smile and his eyes looked like they were in pain. As if he could suddenly feel my presence, he came back to me with a blink of his eyes.

"My wife used to say the same thing. Well, not exactly the same thing, but she would always get so mad when I would use the fancy towels to wash the fire residue off."

He trailed off at the end of the sentence, almost as if he just realized he had spoken those words. A wife. He had a wife, or used to have a wife. Wow. I guess I wasn't the only one who needed to talk tonight.

Knowing that that revelation was something he knew he had to say, but was terrified to say it, I took pity on his frozen form. I gently tugged the washcloth back into my hands, damped it and dabbed at his face. I felt relieved that the water base paint I had chosen was indeed coming off fairly easily. There shouldn't be too much we couldn't rinse off with time.

I rinsed the cloth clean, hung it to dry, took his hand and led him back out into the living room. He still had a dazed and worried look on his face and I wasn't sure my look didn't match his. We were quite the pair.

I settled him down on my amazing L shaped sofa and sat facing him. He sighed deeply and let his head fall back and his eyes close. My heart was breaking. My strong, sweet man looked in agony. So much so, that a single tear was finding its way down his face. I took his hand in mine and began to stroke it softly. With my other hand, I reached up and caught the lone tear and tucked his loose hair off his face. He was lost in a memory and I knew, when he was ready, he would let me in. I wouldn't rush him.

He looked over at me and gave me a sad, lopsided smile. "So, yeah, I had a wife."

I reached out and trailed a finger softly over his eyebrow and gently let it fall down. I was horrible at offering comfort. "Do you want to talk about it?"

He dragged his hands up and over his face. It felt like he was trying to erase my touch there, or else he was just a completely frustrated, done in man. He turned to look me in the eye. "I don't really want to talk about it, but it seems I have to start talking. I wasn't sure when we were going to have this conversation and I'm really sorry, but, I didn't think it was going to be tonight."

"Well, I knew we would be talking, but I thought it would start at some pretty high level obvious issues we were about to face. Then, when I could tell you weren't going to run screaming and crying, I would let you know that I had a wife. A wife that died."

He just left that hanging out there. Wow, a wife. He was a widow. It seemed that we had much more in common than I ever thought. I wasn't a widow, but I was running from a ghost you could say.

"Ok, um, I'm sorry for your loss. How long ago did she pass away?"

"She passed away five years ago." God, he looked miserable. This night wasn't going at all like we had planned.

"How did she die? Or, ah, is that not something you want to talk about?"

"No, I don't want to talk about it, Frankie. I want to let you in, but understand, this isn't going to be easy and most likely won't go so well on my end. Every time I feel like I'm ready to move on and give dating or feeling something for someone a try, she comes back and gets in the way and reminds me of promises made and vows not kept. My story isn't a happy ending, Frankie. She died tragically. And there's kind of more tragedy surrounding her death that blocks me from moving forward nearly every day."

I took his hand and once again tried to shift him towards me. Even a fraction of an inch, but he wasn't budging. He needed to do this his way, so I let him face away from me, for now. Oh how the tables had turned. I started circling my thumb around the pads of his hand in a lame effort to sooth him. His eyes flickered my way for the briefest of moments and I knew he was still with me somewhere in there.

He began again, nervously running the hand I wasn't holding up and through his hair. "So, yeah, well, when she died, she wasn't the only person who died." Another lone tear escaped his eye and travelled a determined path down his face. He made no moved to wipe it away, so neither did I. "She died protecting our son. I had a child. A baby, actually. He was only three months old at the time. She died wrapped around him trying to keep him alive."

Chapter 17

Frankie

The lone tear was now lost amongst a river. I realized at that moment he was here to save me, but, he also needed me to save him. I crawled over onto his lap and forced his face to look at me. He resisted, but I held on.

"I can't Frankie." He mumbled through his agonizing sobs. "I can't do this with you. I don't want you to see this." We sat like that, letting the world around us disappear for this moment in time. We were frozen and holding onto each other for dear life. Slowly, his tears slowed and he looked up into my eyes. The corner of his mouth turned up into a sad smile that I returned. I pulled the sleeve of my shirt down to cover my hand and used it to dab away the remaining tears.

He took a deep breath and released it while lowering his head. He threaded his left hand through my hair and began to weave his fingers through. His other hand held onto my shirt for dear life. "God, I am so sorry, Frankie. I don't know what the hell just happened.

"It's ok, Hardy. I get it."

"Nope, don't think you do. That kind of shit isn't supposed to come out that way. I'm pretty sure I just grew a vagina."

I sputtered, hiccupped and laughed all at once. "I really don't think so." I moved a hand down his rock solid chest. "No, definitely haven't gone all soft on me. Look, shit happens. Stuff like that always comes out when it's not planned or at the most awful times. If you indeed have grown a vagina, you'd just deal with it, hug someone and have a drink. What do you say?"

"I'll take a drink, and the hug for sure and I guess I'll deal with it somehow. But I'm giving back the vagina. God, I can't even say that word without cringing and waiting for the smack on my head from my mom."

I was still seated across him on his lap so he simply reached around and squeezed. It had been a long time since I had been touched like this. I was surprised to notice I wasn't flinching or figuring out a way to run. It was a small step, but a momentous one for me. I even had the bravery to reach up and try to sooth him by trailing my hands through his hair. He had the best hair. And there I went, off again onto a tangent, thinking about Hardy. He ended my daydreams as he loosened his grip on my waist and we let go of each other.

"How about that drink next and I'll sit here and try to deal with it?"

"Sure." I got up and went to the fridge to grab us a drink. Beer for him, water for me. I had a feeling this was only part one of the evening's entertainment. I needed a clear head if I was going to dance around all the feelings in this room.

When I returned, he had gotten himself and his manhood back on track and was looking decidedly less sad. I passed him his beer and sat down beside him, setting my water on the coffee table in front.

"OK, where do we go from that?"

He laughed. "Were you just funny again?"

"I keep telling you I'm funny, Hardy. You've only uncovered the tip of my iceberg."

"I see. Well, I've done enough sharing tonight. I think I'll hand over the microphone to you for a bit."

I winced. "Do you have to? Can't we just sit here and love the sound of silence?"

"We're never going to get anywhere if we don't get this out, babe. Will it make it easier if I ask you some questions?"

"Yes."

"Ok then, I will, but you have to promise me you will answer them honestly."

"Oh, I'm honest. To a fault. But, Hardy, there's a lot I just can't tell you, and I'm not sure if I ever will. I know you just shared possibly the most painful thing about you and your life, but I'm not sure I have that much courage."

"Let's just see where the night takes us, ok?"

"Ok."

"Let's start with the easy stuff first. When's your birthday?"

"July 27."

"Where did you grow up?"

"Just outside of Houston, Texas."

"Hm, wouldn't have pegged you for a Texan." He stared at me and lifted his eyebrow suggestively and I knew the easy questions were on their way out and the next fifteen minutes or longer might kill me. "When did you lose your virginity?"

"Oh My God. That is so not happening. Next question please."

He laughed and it was good to see his dimples again. "Alright, sorry about that one. I'll make it easier on you. First kiss?"

"Third grade. By the fence at the edge of school yard on the ladder that you could use to climb over the wire fence to go home for lunch. His name was Jason and he kissed like a dream."

"Wow, this Jason you speak of left quite the impression."

"You have no idea. Next question."

"Why do you hate to be touched?"

Shit. The first question of many I didn't want to answer. "That's complicated."

"So, uncomplicated it for me."

"I don't know if I can."

"Frankie, if this is going to be something, anything at all, no matter how small or how big, you need to start talking. I like you. I really like you, but there is something inside of me telling me to guard my pride because this girl is going to take me down. So help me uncomplicate things. Start at the beginning."

I began to fidget. Suddenly I had dry scalp, my hands needed a self-massage and I was sure I could see someone shady out my back window.

"Why don't we start with some more specific questions. What was his name?"

"Patrick." Damn, that was so not supposed to come out. "Hardy, I can't. This isn't something that you can just fix by talking to me about it."

"Do you think I don't know that? Do you think I want to fix you? I want to know you. I need to know you. Don't over analyze this Frankie. Just keep going."

I calmed myself down and tried to make my mind up. Either I let him in, or I keep him out. If I let him in, we both might get hurt. If I kept him out, it looked like we both would be hurting as well. Damned if you do and all that jazz.

I took a deep breath and decided, for the first time in my life, I was going to jump.

Chapter 18

Frankie

"Yes, his name is Patrick. I had a relationship with him for many years. We grew up together and our parents expected us to get married at some point. They groomed us for years without us knowing we were puppets in their sick and twisted show. We played together, travelled together and hung out together. We were inseparable, until, one day, we were separated. I went off to study art and he stayed behind to study business and begin to get ready to one day take over his father's business and political empire. During this time period, something in him changed. When we saw each other on breaks, he was wild, erratic and had developed a tendency towards violence. He began to use his fists to settle his disputes."

"Looking back, it was a learned behaviour. I didn't recognize the signs, but they were evident when I began to really watch how his father and mine behaved to our mothers. Dismissive, authoritative and quick to shame them, yet when in the public eye, complimented them, smiled beside them and led them around like a prized horse."

"He began to bug me when I came home and often when I was in New York, about dropping the silliness of getting my degree and move back home where I belonged. I thought it was cute for a while. It was nice to feel loved and wanted, but soon it became obsessive and mean and I came home less and less. Finally, I broke up with him just before I graduated. I admit, I was awful. I did it over the phone. And then I turned my phone off. Look up coward on Google and see my face with there." I began to feel the usual anxiety that accompanied my thoughts of him and that time in our life.

"Do I need to go on?"

"Frankie," he opened his arms. I instantly crawled up into him and wrapped my arms around him. It took one, long deep breath before I was able to relax in his arms. The touching thing was new for me, but I was beginning to see the difference. The difference between different men who touched me. So instead of giving into the fear, I took another tentative step out into the light.

"He showed up at my door one day, banging and yelling at me to open up. My roommates were out and I wasn't sure it was a great idea to let him in, but I did. I did and it was the worst decision I have ever made." My voice cracked and I begged myself not to cry. If it started, I didn't know where or when it would end. One breath in, one breath out. Repeat.

"I opened the door and he barged on in, running me right over. He looked like the perfect business man. Great suit, perfectly starched shirt, opened at the collar to reveal a glimpse of his chest. But I was an educated woman. I had grown up in the school of pretentious assholes. My father was the teacher and here stood before me, his greatest student. He thought he was untouchable. And he was mostly right. He reeked of alcohol. He was slurring his words and was unsteady on his feet. I moved to hold him up and he decided to backhand me into the door." Hardy's arms flinched and in response, I moved to get away, except he firmly, but gently held me in place.

"Frankie, be still. I'm not going to hurt you, baby. You don't need to go on. I think I get the idea."
"No, you don't. Not yet, anyways."
"Well, we can save it for later."

"I don't know if I'll have the strength for a later."
"Ok, well then, go on, but believe me, I'm finding it challenging to sit still. I need to pace and plan."

"Plan what?"

"Plan for the day I meet this guy."
"That's never going to happen. Hardy, he's long gone from my life and that's the way he's going to stay."

All I got was a soft grunt in return and his hand quieting my racing heart by softly taming my hair back from my face.

"Ok, so, yeah, I had never been hit before, but I had definitely watched my mom take a few. But she always went back to him. After a few repeats of this cycle, I lost all respect for her and never had any desire to watch her forgive him time and again. I said I was going to be different and at first, I was. I told him to get out and he reacted as I expected. He apologized over and over again. He tried to come near me to hold me but I screamed at him to get out. Loudly. He finally understood his precious reputation was at stake, and if I continued to cause a scene, the police may get called and so he left. And I didn't see him again for ten glorious years."

This was the part of my story that I needed to be careful with. I had a potential minefield to navigate and blowing up was so not an option. "Then one fateful night, I agreed to go to a party with a friend back in LA. I normally hate parties, but she was stalking a cast mate who she had a huge crush on and needed moral support. So, I spent most of the night, just being creepy and hanging out alone, lurking in the corners. That's how I saw him. He looked pretty different than what I had remembered. I hadn't been home to Texas since that night. See, after I called my mom to tell her we had broken up and that he had hit me, she told me to suck it up and get on with getting married. A good wife had to take a few corrections before she knew exactly how her husband preferred her to act. I pretty much disowned them and cut them from my life. I still haven't touched the trust fund money they have in an account."

"Can we take a break?"

I breathed a sigh of relief and apprehension. I wasn't sure I could get back on track if he needed me to, but still, the night had been an emotional one so a break was probably for the best. "Yeah, sure."

He hopped up from the couch and grabbed my hand and pulled. "Come on, Red. Let's get out of here for a bit." He reached up and cupped my cheeks in his hands and gently scratched me with the pads of his thumbs. He looked like he may just lean in and see what happens, but the indecision must have won. My body was really mad at him, but my brain was thankful. I had no idea what to think at this point. Did he think I was nuts, did he think I was pathetic. I needed to know but was too afraid to ask.

He gave me the saddest half smile and took my hand and pulled me out the front of my house with him.

"Where are we going?"

"Home."

"Home?"

"Yup."

"Not gonna elaborate huh?"

"Nope."

"'Cause, I kinda thought I was home."
He just grabbed my arm and smiled.

Chapter 19

Hardy

God damn. I had to get myself under control before I did something we would both regret. I know it took a lot of guts for her to spill that story, but what did she expect me to do with that information? I was a natural born protector. I couldn't let this go, but she clearly wanted me to.

What I wanted to do was find that asshole and re-arrange his face. I wasn't a violent person. Ever. But the violence that was done to Frankie by this guy made me feel like I was gonna Hulk out or something.

I needed to get her somewhere I felt safe and comfortable before we continued this. I had a feeling the rest of her story was going to get much, much worse. I also needed a mental break. I don't what the hell possessed me to blurt out I had a wife without a care in the world. Jesus, I needed to give my head a shake.

It was out there now, and man, was it ever. I'm sure me bawling like a baby was super hot. That hadn't happened since I lost Sarah. What was it about this woman that had me all crazy? If I was going to be honest with myself, I knew what it was.

She was my second chance at a life by my design. I wasn't the kind of guy to just drift through life, happy without a commitment to speak of. I needed the package. The wife, the kids, the house by the sea, the great job. Everything. I wanted everything and I wanted it with Frankie. I just didn't know how I was going to convince her that everything with me, was what she wanted too.

Chapter 20

Frankie

He opened the passenger door on his truck and I hopped in and buckled up. We turned left and drove along the coast, about five miles, turned down a drive and parked in front of a beautiful ranch home, full of rich wood and weathered siding and inviting stone. It was my perfect idea of a home on the beach. We jogged by it daily and I always daydreamed about who lived inside and what their perfect lives would be like.

Hardy opened my door and helped me down and led me up the path to the front door. And he walked in. And I knew. He was right, this was home.

We walked into the entryway and I started laughing which was saying something considering the mood I had been in just a few moments ago. "Get out! You live here? I love this place. I wanted to rent it but you would obviously know, it wasn't a rental option."

"No, no it wouldn't be. It's mine. I built it with my dad and brother about ten years ago. It was my parent's dream house. They tore down the old house that was on this lot and we built this one. My mom moved to a smaller house when my dad died. I had always intended to move in with my wife and kids, but well, that didn't last for too long.. Anyway, this place, it just feels like home."

"Well, I absolutely love it. Can I get a tour?"

Just then, roaring around the corner, came my arch nemesis, Chuck. He plowed into me once again, begging for my attention. I hunched down, scratched him behind the ears and let him lick me in gratitude.

"Chuck, down." Hardy snapped his fingers and Chuck stopped what he was doing and went to lay down on his bed.

I hooked my arm through his and he lead me forward into an amazing kitchen that spanned nearly the whole mid-section of the house. It was surrounded by windows that looked out onto the beach and the ocean beyond and I could his picture his wife doing dishes at the sink while little Hardys ran around and was hit with a wave of sadness mixed with jealousy so strong I didn't know what to do with it. There was a long and well - loved harvest table to the right of the kitchen, and it too overlooked the beach. Opposite the table was the living area. Gorgeous, completely butter soft, brown leather couches framed an enormous stone fireplace. Framing this centrepiece, were two tall bookshelves jammed full of an eclectic book collection I couldn't wait to browse.

"Hardy, I can't tell you how amazing this house is. I grew up in a mausoleum. This, this is a home with a heart and a living, breathing soul."

He looked at me funny, smiled and pulled me into the hallway leading off the main living space. At the end of the hallway we entered what must be the master bedroom. It was masculine, but not deep woods masculine. Just enough for one to know a man lived here and a man built this house. It had an ensuite and beautiful doors that opened up onto a deck that held an inviting hot tub overlooking the ocean.

We quickly toured the rest of the house, which held a couple more bedrooms, a bathroom and a utility room and then circled back to sit in front of the fireplace. It was a cool night and so Hardy set about building a small fire in the fireplace and I sat there, mesmerized. Watching him move was fascinating. He was wearing a simple t-shirt and jeans, but he moved around with the grace of a man who knew who he was, where he was going and how he was going to get there. He must have been magic to watch fight fires. Naked. I covered my mouth with my hand and let out a giggle. Where in the hell did that come from?

I knew where it came from. It wasn't a stretch to get there from where I was at that moment. But to actually think it aloud in my head was hilarious and if I didn't watch myself, pretty soon, he was going to think I was a lunatic.

He finished the fire and got up and turned and smiled. His smile was slowly coming back to full wattage. Not long now, unless I screwed things up as I probably was only moments away from doing.

"Drink?"

"Sure, just water please."

He went to the kitchen and grabbed us both a drink of water and returned to sit on the couch. I suddenly got nervous. I felt like I was 15 and on my first date again. We were already miles ahead with the sharing than I ever was at fifteen, but still, I think I was needing another coat of deodorant.

He decided to take pity on me and be the first to talk. "Ok, I think we've done enough sharing for one night. Let's table the rest of our stories for another night."

"Well, I don't know. I kind of feel like I need to finish. Before, um, well." My voice just trailed off. I really wasn't sure what the next steps were for us, but I did know he needed to know what he was dealing with before we went any further.

"Before what, Red?"

"Are you really going to make me say it?"

He smiled, finally, a dimpled, all in smile. "Yeah, I think I am."

"Well, um-"

Just then, we were interrupted by the loud and obnoxious and anxiety inducing sound of his pager.

"Shit. I'm sorry Frankie. I've got to go. Quickly. Can I just drop you at your door?"

"Yes, of course. But you don't have to do that. I can call a cab."

We got up and hurried towards the door. "Not at damn chance you're doing that, babe." We went out the front door and he firmly led me with a hand at my back, towards his truck. "Hop in." And with that, he gave me a little shove into his truck and we took off like a bat out of hell, heading towards an unknown fire.

We lurched to a stop in front of my house and I turned to him, frustrated we had to end our night early and terrified of a fire dangerous enough to pull him in on his night off.

"Be careful, please."

"Always."

I turned to open the door, when he grabbed my arm. As per usual, my reflexes took over and I physically went slack, assuming that when anyone grabbed be like that, it was in anger. Hardy just looked at me, his eyebrows nearly touching he was frowning so bad.

"That's gonna stop, Red. And when we have a minute, we're gonna finish your story. Babe, I'm not him. But I know, it's not time yet. You need to get used to this idea, and I need to get to work. I'll text you later, k?"

"Please. I'll worry." And that was that. I hopped down and bolted into my house.

I locked the door behind me and sunk down to the ground. If I was going to be successful at rejoining normal society, I was going to have to get a hold of myself in situations such as these. Hardy grabbing me on my arm was a totally normal thing to do. Walking in the dark from a car to my door, also normal. What wasn't normal? My reactions.

I picked myself up and dragged myself to the bathroom to wash my face and get ready for bed. It was my routines that made me feel normal. I needed to know what was coming next. So, next for me was bed. I set my cell beside my bed frowning when I didn't see a text alert.

Right Frankie. He hardly had the time to get to the fire, let alone text you. He was fine. And so was I. And yes, now I was talking to myself. A sign of not being alright. I drifted off into a restless sleep, dreaming of dark and fire and fear.

Chapter 21

Frankie

I bolted upright a few hours later when my phone alert let me know I had an incoming call. It was Hardy.

"Hi." My voice sounded groggy and it took me a few minutes to clear my brain.

"Hi, sorry to wake you, but, babe, do you think I could come over? Nothing funny's going to happen, I just need to sleep beside someone tonight."

His voice held the weight of the world and even though I wasn't sure I was ready, I knew I couldn't deny him this small request.

"Yes, of course you can."

"Thanks. I'm in your driveway."

"Stalker. I'll be right there. Meet me at my door."

I hung up and padded my way to the back door, not really paying attention to what I was wearing. I opened the door and there he was. Dressed in his uniform, dirty, hair messed and full of black dirt. I couldn't have cared less. His face held a pain that was my undoing. He needed me right now and that was a miracle in itself. This brave, strong man, needed me. Who'd have thought?

I went to him and felt him fall. I held him in a hug as best I could. I shuffled him inside and we collapsed onto the floor. It was then I realized he was sobbing. His whole body was taking part in the process. He wept openly for a few minutes, then I heard him speak through his tears.

"I lost someone tonight. It was bad, Frankie. So bad. I don't know how to deal with it."

"You'll get through it sweetheart. You can do this."

"You don't understand. They died, Frankie. My wife and son, they died. In a fire that I couldn't put out in time to save them. I killed them."

I didn't know what to say. I was horrible at giving comfort to begin with and now to hear this final piece of his story, I didn't know how to react. I just started to cry. Our stories were so full of pain and suffering and we were living with it for what looked like the rest of our miserable lives.

All I could think to do was to pick him up. "Hardy, sweetheart, let's get you up and you can fall apart somewhere more comfortable." He apparently had other ideas. As I tried to haul him up, he pulled me down. We ended up in a shaking heap on the floor, my arms wrapped around him. I gave up trying to move us and just decided to trust my instincts.

I sat him up and leaned him up against my wall. I spread his legs out and arranged myself, facing him, in between his legs. I lifted my legs up and over his legs and skooched forward so we were face to face and body to body and wrapped my arms around him and hung on. My tears had stopped but he seemed to still be struggling with his grief.

His body shook each time he dragged a breath in and he occasionally choked on a sob. I decided talking about what had happened was going to wait. He would be ready when he was ready and I needed to get past all my issues and let the focus shift. We hung on to each other for another ten minutes or so. He was so quiet I thought maybe he had fallen asleep.

"One night, I was at the station. I was at the station a lot. I was fairly new and always volunteered for extra shifts if I could. We needed the money and I needed the experience. We had just had a baby. A boy. His name was Jacob. He was three months old, and my wife was going to have to go back to work if we didn't find out a way to earn a little more money. Staying home was really important to her."

Oh God. We were going to do this. I was so not sure I was ready for this conversation. I was so shitty at this kind of thing and Hardy was in so much pain. As if he knew what I was thinking, he tightened his hold on me and gave me a short squeeze. And carried on.

"So, there I was, eager idiot. Fooling around at the firehouse when a call came in. A house, on Eagle Drive, full on fire. I realized immediately that it could be our house and panicked. I grabbed my gear and started screaming at the team to give me the house number. No one would and I realized why. I wasn't going to this fire. I wasn't able to work a fire at my own home and if they gave me the house number, I might end up beating them there and race inside not thinking straight. But none of that mattered to me. I knew when they didn't tell me, it was my address and I took off way before they could.

I pulled up to the house and started screaming. I knew. I knew it was already too late. We lived in an old home while we were renovating the beach house. It was an electrical fire. They were down in the basement, doing laundry. The fire had blocked the stairs and the windows on the basement level were too small for anyone to fit through. Didn't matter. They were old and didn't open. She tried to break one open. She had managed to get one window pretty much clear of glass, but it must have already been too late. The smoke had damaged Jacob's lungs to the point of no return. She followed shortly after. The call to 911 hadn't come in until the house was already fifty percent burned. By the time anyone got there, it was nearly gone. Of course, I didn't think. I ran in anyway. I didn't care two shits about my life. I just needed to get my family out to safety."

"I ran in but was met with a wall of pure flame. I tried to move forward, but a pair of arms grabbed me from behind and dragged me back outside. I was tackled to the ground and held there by my chief while the other guys went in. I put up a good fight but knew he wouldn't move. After thirty agonizing minutes they finally came out holding my family. My lifeless, tiny little family."

He sobbed a breath in and I felt the wetness of the tears rolling down my face. "I'm sorry, Hardy. So, so very sorry." I tried to calm him with my hands in his hair and my shushing noises. "Oh, baby. I'm so very sorry." My voice was just a whisper and I wasn't even sure he was hearing me, but this was about all I knew to do.

We sat and stayed in this pattern for another ten minutes or so until one of us finally needed to be brave enough to look the other in the eyes. Up until this point, we hadn't been looking at each other and that had made it so much easier. Of course, Hardy had done all the hard work. It wasn't my time, but I knew that after tonight, it would be my story's turn very soon.

I pulled my head back and gently detached myself from his embrace and tried to assess the damage. My shirt was soaked, but otherwise, neither of us looked any worse for wear. I took Hardy's face in my hands and smiled at him. "Thank-you for sharing that with me."

He just looked back at me. "I'm sorry I left my balls at the door. This was so not how I wanted to tell you. I'm pretty embarrassed right now."

I kept my hands in place and squeezed a little harder. "Are you for real right now? From what I can tell, your balls are still firmly in place and I couldn't give two shits about your manhood. That took a lot of guts right there and that's a more manly move than most men I know."

He rested his forehead against mine and sighed deeply. "Red, can I stay here tonight? I promise, nothing will happen, I just, I need someone to be with me."

I hesitated. This was huge for me. I knew he didn't mean stay with me tonight in the guest bedroom. He meant stay with me, beside me, in my bed. I hadn't allowed that to happen yet and wasn't sure I could handle it.

He must have sensed my hesitation. "Forget it. I know it's too much to ask. I'm sorry Frankie. I didn't mean to push you too far." He hauled himself up, swiped a hand around his eyes and walked to the door.

I knew this moment was mine to blow and it looked like I was totally going to fulfill that prophecy. Damn! How long was I going to let that asshole take things away from me? "Stay." I practically shouted it at him. "Please, Hardy. Stay. With me. Here, in my house, in my bed, tonight." Oh God. I think I was going to barf. I ran past him, to the bathroom and tried to do just that. I felt him come up behind me and wrap his arms around me from behind.

"Shhh, baby. Relax. I'm not him. Let's get you cleaned up and into bed."

"I'm sorry, Hardy."

"Nope, not gonna hear it. Brush those barfy teeth and let's get to bed. I am fucking exhausted. You must be too."

He waited patiently for me to brush and rinse and stall as long as I could without blowing my cover. Then he steered me towards my bedroom and it was just then I realized that I was dressed for bed. In my tank top. And thong. Jesus, why me? How was I going to covertly put on some more clothes without looking like I was putting on some more clothes?

I ended up having no choice in the matter. He ushered me into bed, expertly tucked me in, on my side no less, and proceed to strip down to his boxer briefs in no time flat. I hardly had any time to admire the sight before me, than he pulled the covers back and hopped in. Since I was still in a state of stunned silence, he raised an eyebrow, decided better of it, reached over me and switched off my bedside light. The whole time of which, I laid still as a statue, just ogling him.

He must have got his balls back from the front door, as he snaked an arm underneath me, grabbed a hold of my waist and flipped me onto my other side, facing away from him. He scooted up behind me and laid his other hand around me, effectively spooning me and trapping me.

"Relax. This is it, babe. I don't yet know what's got a hold of you in that gorgeous head of yours, but I will get it out. I need you tonight and I know you can do this for me." He tucked my hair behind me ear and I could feel his warm, soothing breath behind it. I can do this. I so cannot do this. Shit, I can do this.

My internal argument lasted for ten seconds then exhaustion won. His soothing strokes and relaxing murmuring soothed my anxiety and I began to get sleepy fairly soon after. I would be lying to myself if I didn't admit it felt nice to be held without the threat of violence by the hottest guy I had ever known. I smiled a secret smile and started to doze. I swore on my life I heard Hardy say, "you're mine now Red. I'm not ever letting you go, baby."

But that would be too much for me to handle right now, so I just convinced myself it never happened and drifted off to sleep.

Chapter 22

Frankie

I woke to the smell of bacon, which I had no idea I even owned, and coffee. That of which I definitely owned. I had no idea how to proceed. I slept beside a man last night. In safety, not fear. This was new territory for me and something I had told myself wasn't going to happen for a long time, if ever again. I had to move soon. I had used up my allotted time here and needed to make a move before he found me again. I guess it was time to finish the talk. Hardy needed to know where I stood. It was only fair.

I blew my errant hair out of my face and heaved my tired body out of bed. I slipped on some yoga pants and zipped up a hoody over my tank and set out to find the food. Along the way, I decided to detour into the bathroom to take care of a few things and brush my teeth. Just in case. I laughed at myself. In case of what, moron. I had better make my mind up of what I wanted and needed from Hardy before too long.

I found him in my tiny kitchen cooking eggs and bacon and brewing coffee. He turned when I walked in and his face registered a mix of happiness and anxiety.

"Morning. I made you breakfast to make up for last night." He began to plate the eggs, fried, just the way I loved them. Sunnyside up. "Sunnyside up eggs, side of dry toast and bacon."

I smiled at him and felt another crack in my terrified heart. This man was amazing. I wish our circumstances were different. There was no way anything with him would go anywhere, but I was trying to keep up the courage to live in the moment.

"Thanks, Hardy. You didn't have to do this? Don't you have to work today?"

"Yes, I did and yes, I do. Frankie, just let me, please. I totally lost it on you last night and this is just a small sample of the amount of gratitude I have for you. You overcame some of your own massive issues last night for my sake and I want you not know how much that meant to me. Now, sit and eat so I can head out to work. Then, when I'm done, we're going on a proper date."

"Oh, I don't think-"

"Nope, no thinking from now on. Just moving forward. For both of us. Please, Frankie. Just let me take you out on a real live date. The two of us. Somewhere out of town where no one knows us so we won't get hassled. I'll pick you up at six. Now, eat."

He picked up a fork and shovelled some eggs into my mouth and pushed my jaw up and down to simulate chewing. I guess I had no choice in the matter. It looked like I was going on a date and I was eating my weight in calories for breakfast.

"That's my girl. Now, I've got to run. I still have to head home to get a change of clothes and pick up Chuck from the dog sitter. Tonight, we're gonna talk about the messed up shit I did last night and then we are going to move on." He brushed past me, jerked to a halt, turned back to face me and lightly kissed my temple. He rested a moment there and it felt like he had more to say. He must have changed his mind, as he smiled a sad smile and spun on his heel and left.

Left with no other options other than to eat my breakfast or stew over my impending date tonight, I decided to eat first, then stew, then run, then stew some more.

The doorbell rang promptly at six and I gave my outfit one last look. I didn't have a lot of going out clothing options. I pretty much left the majority of that part of my wardrobe behind and since then, had no need to replace any of it. I had made do tonight with dark, dressy skinny jeans, a flowy, emerald green silk tank and a pair of nude wedge heels. I left my hair down, but had managed to blow it out straight with some added beach type waves. I grabbed my clutch and ran to cut him off at the door before he wandered in and made himself at home.

I pulled open the door and could only imagine the shock registering on my face. Hardy looked hot in jogging shorts. Hardy looked unbelievable in his uniform, but this Hardy standing before me took old Hardy to a whole new level.

He was wearing navy dress pants, with a crisp white collared shirt underneath and his unruly chestnut hair was slicked straight back and to the side a little. His collar was open enough to reveal a light dusting of hair and a glimpse at some amazingly outlined pecs. His was clean shaven and I longed to touch his face to confirm it was as soft as it looked to be. He looked like he fit right in on Wall Street and I had to really make an effort to school the shock I felt and ensure it didn't translate onto my face.

"You look fantastic. That green is amazing on you."

"Hardy, I'm so underdressed. You didn't tell me it was a dressy place."

"It isn't."

"Then why are you so dressed up?"

"'Cause I like dressing up? Look, doesn't matter what we're wearing. It's a casual pub type dining place, but I wanted you to see a different side of me. A side that actually wears clothes that were flammable and not fire and sweat resistant."

"So, I shouldn't change?"

"No way." He held out his arm. "You chariot awaits, Madame."

"Why, thank you kind sir."

He helped me up into his truck and I realized that no matter where we were going, taking his truck to get there would always take the formality down a notch or two.

We drove for about twenty minutes out of town until we came to a small village down the coast. We made small talk and danced around most of the stuff we really needed to talk about. I was thankful it appeared we were finally at our destination so I could stop trying to think of things to say that sounded remotely intelligent.

We pulled up at a restaurant called Ocean and parked in the nearly full parking lot. I hopped down before he could make it around to my side. I needed to stay in control of this evening's events. When he touched me, I tended to forget what it was I needed to focus on.

We walked in and I quickly realized it was the type of place where any kind of attire really worked. The restaurant was divided into two main areas. To our left was the bar and to the right was the area for food service. The rooms were decorated with warm, polished wood and the seating was eclectic, mis-matched bench and chair seats. Polished brass accented the room all around.

The hostess led us to our table. We had scored a secluded corner table where no one could see my sure to be embarrassing reactions to the things we were going to talk about.

We sat and ordered some drinks and as soon as the server left us, Hardy decided to jump right into it.

"Ok, want to tell me why you've been so quiet? Why you're not answering any of my questions?"

"What are you talking about? I'm just tired today."

"Come on Frankie. That's bullshit. Why don't you just spit it out so we can enjoy our dinner and move on with the night."

"That's just it, Hardy. What I need to say will destroy our night. So, I would rather we enjoyed our night and talked about the hard stuff later."

"We're always talking about things later. And then shit like last night happens. So, I think we'll start talking now, and then we can save the evening afterwards."

"Hardy, I don't think-"

"Yup, there you go. Just stop. We've had this conversation before. Stop thinking."

"Ugh, but, it's not that easy. There are things and people that need protection from the stuff I need to say. And there's a better than good chance that I will lose my shit in here, in front of all these people during this conversation, so I would prefer if we could wait and do it in private."

He smiled and took my hand. He stared at it while he began to draw light circles around the delicate skin between my finger and thumb. He smiled a private smile and then looked up. Oh God, I was so screwed.

"Ok, Red. Here's what we're gonna do instead. It's twenty questions for you, or a tell all. Take your pick."

"That's not fair. That's just another way for you to get the information you want."

"Nah, I'll just ask you stupid stuff. If it gets too personal, you can take a pass without me complaining."

"I don't know."

"Well, I could also play twenty dirty questions. Would that be better?"

I spit out the water that I was trying to drink. I started choking and gasped and was sure this was going to be the worst first date in the history of first dates. "No, regular twenty questions will work just fine thanks."

He smiled an evil grin. "I knew you'd come around. But for the record, dirty questions is still going to happen. Just not tonight."

"In your dreams, buddy."

"Always." His face turned serious and his eyes became heated and it was the reminder I needed to get back on track for plan A. My plan had no real plan within it, but I was sure it was solid nonetheless.

The waitress came and took our order and Hardy clapped his hands together and raised his left eyebrow and smirked. "Ready? Let's get started."

I knew I wasn't ready, but I couldn't put him off much longer so I might as well get whatever was going to happen over with. "Sure, ready."

"Hm, let's see. Do you have any siblings?"

I tried to let all emotions and issues leaving my face before I began answering his questions. "No, only child."

"Where did you grow up?"

"Texas. You asked me that already."

"How old are you?"

"Thirty-five."

"Before you retired to the eastern seaboard at the ripe old age of thirty-five, what did you do?"

"Well, to pay the bills, I was an art historian. I am also an artist. A painter to be specific."

"I figured as much. Your work is beautiful."

I ducked my head and felt my cheeks grow heated. It was never easy to take a compliment and even less so after spending so many months being ridiculed for any attention I received and then paying for it in the privacy of our home at night. Patrick was a jealous man and any praise I received did not sit well with him.

I felt a calloused finger beneath my chin, gently encouraging me to lift my head. He smiled and I looked anywhere but in his eyes. "Frankie, look at me please."

"Why?"

"Just, please?"

I was so out of my league here. I didn't do eye contact. I didn't trade secrets. This was asking too much. I kept my gaze away from his.

"Fine," he said. "Let's continue. I'll keep it simple, but know that it's going to get harder as we go. What's your favourite colour?"

"Blue."

"Favourite drink?"

"Water."

"Water?"

"Yup, water. I know, so lame. Want to end the date now?"

"No, it's just that I've never met someone who's favourite drink was water. That was rather unique. Ok, let's see. Where do I go after water?"

"Ha, ha." He had picked up my hand again and was playing with my fingers. It was such an easy thing to do, but it was so strange to me. Had I really forgotten how it was to be with someone who wasn't a monster?

His eyes suddenly shifted to the left, slanted in concern and his hand stopped it's playful wanderings.

"What's wrong?" I asked.

He flicked his gaze back to me. "Nothing."

"Liar."

"Really, nothing. Just could have sworn there was a guy I had seen around over there. I also could have sworn he was staring us down."

A feeling of unease slowly crept coldly up my spine. "What did he look like?' I tried to talk as normally as I could. There was no way my ex had found me, but it was always smart to be aware of him possibly being close to finding me. George and Sam kept fairly close tabs on him, however, he was a sneaky bastard and I wouldn't put it past him to get by their radar.

"Just a regular guy," Hardy went on, oblivious to my distress. "Dark hair, tallish, dressed nicely."

That could have been anyone. Shit, it could have been Hardy. Dinner came at that moment and it was the distraction we both were looking for.

We paused our game and indulged in small talk while we ate. I listened as Hardy told me hilarious stories about his team and I couldn't help but ruin my reputation as a cold hearted bitch during some of his stories of the shit they got up to while waiting to rescue the next person in distress.

"There it is again," Hardy said.

"What?"

"You do laugh. Does it hurt? You don't use that skill very often."

My mouth hung open in mock dismay. "Wow, Hardy. You really know how to treat a girl. It's a wonder I haven't jumped you on this table here in the middle of the restaurant."

He laughed that amazing, full on laugh. I wondered after last night how he did that. How did he seem to be able to find such joy in the truths of life. Maybe if I slept with him, I could get a little of that joy for myself. I mentally slapped my inner whore. When in the hell had she woken up? She needed to go back to wherever she was hiding out, before I really did jump Hardy on this very table.

"Babe, if you're going to get anything from me, it's complete honesty. I'm an open book, just ask. So, when I say I've never seen frowning come in a sexier package, believe me. However, I love to hear you laugh and see you smile. Just once in a while. We don't need to go changing things too drastically."

"I don't know whether to be completely insulted or incredibly turned on."

"I know what I would choose."

"How do you do it Hardy?"

"Do what?"

"Live. With joy in your heart."

"Ah, I see you get to choose when we talk about the heavy stuff, but I can't."

"I'm sorry. I didn't mean to. I didn't even think."

"There, see how easy not thinking was? I didn't mean I wasn't going to answer you, but I think you were right. It's an answer best left for later tonight."

"Fair enough. Let's finish eating then, shall we?"

He smiled, but I could see the sadness in his eyes. I had done that. Once again, I had screwed up. We ate the rest of our meal in relative silence, both of us retreating to our corners to mull over what could happen to our delicate friendship should we spill our guts tonight. It didn't matter. I needed to be honest with him, however, I also was trying to be honest with myself. And this self was completely attracted to that guy. There were a few problems with this.

First off, I hadn't been intimate, even kissed a guy in a year and thanks to my evil ex, I have issues with intimacy. Second, Hardy had a wife and child who died tragically. I'm no therapist, but I am betting he comes with issues as well. Third, I needed to move on from here. My ex was sneaky, connected and wealthy and wouldn't stop until I was no longer a threat. Moving around was the only thing keeping me one step ahead of him. I couldn't get involved with anyone. Ever again. I might be looking at a lifetime of hookups. God, that was depressing. I was hardwired for long term relationships. When I was five I had started to plan my wedding. I couldn't risk it anymore, but I had a feeling Hardy was going to make that break from him a huge issue and I wasn't sure if I was strong enough to weather that storm.

So, I think I was going to look at our time together like a mini romance. I had never experienced a fling and it felt like high time to give myself this life experience. If we could just get past issues one and two that is.

We finished dinner without any other incidents or crazies staring at us and headed back out into the night. It was nice to be out with Hardy where everyone didn't know who he was. Everyone was always friendly enough but I couldn't help but feel their animosity. Hardy was the town hero and the women's dream come true. Gorgeous, tortured soul, who every girl wanted to help him forget about his grief and every guy wanted to hang out and drink beer with him. It was nice to have him all to myself without any judgey eyes on me.

He slipped his hand into mine as we took a walk along the boardwalk over the dunes behind the restaurant. I felt like a teenager again. Re-learning how to be with a man. Experiencing the thrill of a hand held and bodies occasionally bumping into each other as we walked.

"So," he started. "Talking here or somewhere else with four walls and a door you can storm out and lock me out with?"

"Wow, issues much"
"No, just have had some bad experiences so I prefer to talk to a woman about potentially hazardous issues outdoors where she doesn't have an escape route."

"Hazardous issues?"

"And, looks like I already started. Shit, I'm sorry Red." He stopped walking and turned me to face him. As usual, my challenged hair was flying in both our faces from the ocean breeze. He grabbed it and secured it back with one hand. Thus, ingeniously moving a little closer to me. "Listen," he lowered his voice. "I don't want to screw this up like I usually do. Since Sarah died, I haven't done so well on the dating front and I like you." He grabbed a stray hair and held it back with his other hand, now having slyly maneuvered both hands to my head. "I like you a lot."

Shit. He was close. Really, really close and I wasn't sure my well laid plans were all that well laid. They sucked as a matter of fact. Plans to get close to Hardy were dumb. Stupid. Gah. He was leaning in. Shit, shit, shit. This was it. We were in fast forward. Dating, hand holding and now it looked like a kiss all in the past two hours. It was too much to handle.

"I can see your panic, babe," he whispered. "Shush now. Don't worry." He wove his fingers through my hair. It was like calming a skittish horse. God, did I just refer to myself as a horse? He had totally fried my brain cells. They were firmly in sex mode. It wasn't doing good things to my awesome judgement.

I closed my eyes, relaxing into his touch. He continued to shush me, whispering into my ear. "If it makes you feel any better, I'm fucking shitting myself I'm so nervous."

I opened my eyes. "Why?"

He rested his forehead onto mine. "I've kissed girls since my wife died, but I've never kissed someone that meant something to me. Who I could see myself kissing again, and again, and again."

"Oh."

"Yeah, oh. And I have a mixed bag of excitement and guilt, babe. I'm gonna need something from you in order to move this forward."

Fuck it. I opened my eyes, grabbed a hold of shirt with both hands and moved us forward. We crashed into each other, holding on with both hands. He moved to take control of the kiss and I gave him the angle he was searching for. His tongue slid over my lower lip and I opened my mouth to sigh and he invaded. As the kiss went on, we both became bolder. I knew Hardy wasn't going to hurt me and my body was way ahead of me on that one.

Hi hands were firm on both of my cheeks and locked in place, but mine were restless. They were on a mission, resting on his glorious chest wasn't going to be enough for them. I let them slide around his body and down until they found a new and irresistible resting place. His ass. Oh, wow, it was a fine ass. Hard curves and totally grabbable. Asses were always my thing and this one pretty much took the prize.

I'm pretty sure I let out a massive groan at this point, but if anyone asked, I would swear it was him. The kiss escalated to another level and we both realized that our ingenious plan to be outside was backfiring. It wouldn't be long before we were outed for indecent exposure.

I reluctantly pealed my hands off his rear end and pulled away. "Wow."

He smiled. "Yeah, wow. Are you ok?"

I just nodded. Stupid, damn female hormones. I was not crying. No fucking way.

He still had a hold on my face. He tilted me up to look at him. "Hey, what's going on? Talk to me."

"I don't know, Hardy." Oh great. Now I was full on crying. "I'm so embarrassed."

"Why?"

"I don't cry. It's not me. Well, it used to be me, but the new me doesn't cry. This just took me by surprise."

"I know. Me too. Well, that kiss has starred in lot of my alone time lately-" I smacked him in the arm. "Ow, honesty, remember?"

"Too much honesty sometimes is just not cool."

"Ok, anyway, even though I had thought about kissing you quite often," he raised his eyebrows gaging my acceptance, "I still wasn't expecting what just happened."

I smacked him again, but my heart wasn't in it. I had done it. I had kissed a man, who I was attracted to and he didn't hit me, make me feel like shit or take more than what I wanted to give. He had stopped when I was ready. I couldn't wipe the moronic grin off my face.

He grabbed my hand, sending warmth and electricity up my arm, and led me back towards his truck. "Come on. Let's go back to your place and get talking. Or would you prefer my place?"

"Let's go to your place. We always seem to be at my place. Are you on call tonight?"
"I'm always on call. Sorry. But tonight, the guys have explicit instructions to only call if they can't handle the situation. We may get lucky." He wiggled his eyebrows suggestively.

"Oh my God. Groan!"

He dropped my hand to wind it around my waist and hug me to him. It was a simple gesture, but so sweet I almost started crying again. We made it back to his truck and he opened my door for me and went around to his side. As I was hauling myself up into my seat the hairs on the back of my neck suddenly stood at attention. I whipped my head around but saw nothing. Still, I couldn't help but feel like something was out there.

I flopped into the seat and shook it off. Hardy started the truck, grabbed my hand and we headed back to an evening of who the hell knew what. I was safe for now, but it wouldn't pay for me to get too comfortable. I needed to talk to Hardy tonight. Before we went any further, he had to know my story and the reasons we would never last.

Chapter 23

Hardy

As we were driving home, my phone alerts were letting me know I had a pile of texts coming in. I was on call, as I was nearly all the time, but these weren't emergency alerts. These were annoying texts from some other source. I wasn't really a technology guy, so I kinda just let the beeping go in one ear and out the other.

"Aren't you going to see who that is?" Frankie obviously was a tech kind of girl. It looked like she wanted to grab the phone and see what the hell was up.

"Nah. I'm driving. Whoever it is can wait."

"If you say so." A mischievous grin started to creep across her face. I had to really concentrate on the road when that happened. She was stingy with her smiles, however, the reason behind it had me on edge.

"Don't touch that phone, Red."

"Wouldn't dream of it."

"Bullshit."

The smile grew wide and she lunged for the phone. I had no idea who it was texting me, but there was a pretty good chance it would either embarrass the shit out of me or put me in the dog house. I hadn't even made it into the house yet, and there was no way I was getting kicked out before I made it to third base.

The problem was, I was driving and she was not. "Lightening quick reflexes there Frankie. You've been holding back on me on our runs?"

She stuck her tongue out at me in answer and swiped on my phone. Lucky for me, I had a tech whiz for a sister who forced me to put a password on the damn thing. It was my turn to stick out my tongue.

"Mature, Hardy."

"Ah, pot meet kettle?"

She pouted and looked all cute and stuff and I almost caved and gave her my password. Then, something occurred to me. "1177"

She looked at me and tilted her head to the side. "What?"

"That's the password. 1177"
And then she got me. I imagined building a life with this woman was going to be a long journey in building trust and I had to start somewhere.

"Hardy. Thank-you."

"Whatever you need, baby, you can get it from me. Ok?"

She smiled that smile and it was all I needed. Well, for now.

She set the phone back in the cup holder. "Not gonna look, Red?"

"Do you want me to?"

"Sure, if you want. I have nothing to hide."

She picked the phone back up and swiped it open, entered the password and grinned. "You have five new texts. Three from Will, one from your sister and one from your mom." She looked over at me. "Do you want to me to read them?"

"If you want."

I could see the indecision she struggled with as she began chewing on her lip. "Ok, only because we've come this far. We might as well see what they wanted."

She turned towards me and couldn't stop grinning like a fool. She had come so far since we first met. My little Red.

"Ok, so, your mom wants to know if you're coming for dinner this week. Your sister wants to know the same thing so she can make sure she's there and she's heard a rumour about you dating some new chick she wants to confirm."

"Hm, wonder what I'll tell her?"

"Yes, I wonder." She looked back down at the phone and snorted. "Looks like Will has heard the same thing. And he has spies at the restaurant who told him we were there. Oh, and he thinks you're getting lucky tonight, but didn't quite use those words."

I grabbed at the phone. "I knew this could have gone bad, quickly."

"Relax, Hardy. Take me home."

Chapter 24

Frankie

"Want a drink?" Hardy asked.

"I'll have whatever you're having."

We were settling into his fantastically comfortable sofa, with a blazing fire. Chuck was snoring softly on his bed off to the side, done in by a day of bouncing around at the beach. It was a setting right out of a romance novel.

"I'm having a beer."

"Sure, I'll have a beer, please." He raised an eyebrow.

"I need something more than water tonight."

He joined me on the sofa and I scooted as far away from him as possible. I needed zero points of contact in order to accomplish my goal tonight.

He looked at me, questioning my location. "Do I have an odour problem I'm going to need to see to?"

I laughed a completely nervous and full of shit laugh. "No, I just can't be close enough to touch you. It will completely distract me from my mission."

"Ah. Well, by all means, let's begin. Who's going first?"

"I am."

I took a huge breath and an even huger gulp of beer. If there was ever a time to turn to liquid courage, this was it.

"So, where did I leave off? Let me think."

I was stalling. Jeez, girl. Rip that band aid off. Just start at the very beginning.

"So, it's ten years later and I see him across the room, chatting to a few people. One of them my friend. I cursed my eternal bad luck, threw back a shot of courage, and walked over join my friend. Our eyes meet and he smiles. Like, smiled from his soul. He had never smiled like that at me before. He looked happy and at peace and I didn't know what to do with this new version of him.

"Frances, he murmured. I had always hated that name, but for some unknown reason, he insisted on calling me by it. He was charming, smooth and had all the right words. He was a changed man he said. He had spent years in therapy turning his life around. He took an interest in the people he was talking to and all the while, kept a closer eye on me. I didn't know what to do with the new Patrick. Somehow, I began to convince myself what he had been like before, was maybe my fault."

"Frankie-"

"No, I know now it wasn't, but then, I wasn't so sure of myself. I didn't have a support system to show me the way people normally were with each other. All I had was my parents and their friends who were all in loveless, abusive relationships."

Shame descended over me and I wasn't sure moving onto the middle of my story was going to be something I could do. I stared into the fire and took myself somewhere else. I felt his presence beside me. He had shifted closer. He reached under me and untucked my legs and planted them across his lap. He sat beside me now. He reached out and traced my cheeks with his fingers. "You don't have to go on tonight if you don't want to."

"I know, but there are some things I need you to understand before I get to the things that you won't understand."

He smiled. "That makes a ton of sense."

I laughed, but my heart wasn't in it. "Well, so, as you may have guessed, we began to see each other again. We went for dinners, walks, to the movies and stayed in. He never once lost his temper and never once made a move to lay a hand on me unless I had invited him to. He was, for intents and purposes, the perfect boyfriend. But things slowly changed and I slowly started to make excuses for him again."

"He began to separate me from my friends. He began to dictate the clothes I wore and the way I styled my hair. He began to argue with me about the little things and then about the big things. I saw it, but didn't really see it, you know? He mixed it all up with tenderness, kindness and sex. I got confused and then ended up doing everything I could to keep those tender moments alive. I made excuses, I bent to his will, I eagerly drew him back in with sex. And eventually, when he landed his first hit, I blamed myself."

A tear threatened to roll down my face. It wasn't time to shed tears anymore. I hadn't told this story to anyone. A few knew the story, but none had heard my firsthand account of how I was an abused woman. Hardy shifted slightly and scooped me up and slid underneath me. He turned my legs so the rested on top of his and I was tucked into the crook of his arm.

"I blamed myself for twelve long months. To the outsiders looking in, we were the perfect pair. To the insiders, we were headed for disaster. Only Sam and Frankie knew what was happening, but I wouldn't listen to them. In hindsight, I needed to make the decision to leave on my own from my own signals. But still, looking back, I feel so much shame about how I treated those woman. It was inexcusable. They are the reason I'm still here."

At this point, my tear pushed through and landed in his lap. "Sorry. I didn't mean to start sobbing all over you."

He lifted my chin to look up at him. "Please stop. Not crying, but trying to be perfect. You're hurting. Your body is releasing it's grief. It's nothing to be embarrassed about. Do you want to keep going?"

"No," I laughed. "But this is the part I need you to hear."

He brushed some of my hair back and gently kissed my temple. "Ok, then, let's see this all the way."

"Well, the abuse began to escalate. We had been dating, then became engaged. I had become an expert at hiding what he was doing to me and basically was a recluse. He is kind of high profile, so had a lot of public engagements to attend. He rarely took me. He always said that he didn't want other men touching what was his. It was easier to agree, but for some reason, one night, I decided to defy him. Well, he didn't know I was defying him, but still, it was a big thing for me."

Deep breath in Frankie, I told myself. The subject matter was about to get tricky. "So, one night, he was out at a party. I decided to follow him and see what the hell he was up to all the time without me. I was beginning to suspect him of cheating on me."

"So, I got it in my stupid head to follow him and maybe catch him doing something that would give me the excuse I needed to leave him. And yeah, I know how pathetic that sounds. I should have been able to pack my bags and walk out the door, but I couldn't. I had become my mother. I had turned into the one person I swore I never would and I knew. I knew then how she had let it happen. She didn't let it happen, she became trapped by her reality and terrified to disrupt it."

I took a break and dared to look over at him. He was looking at me with curiosity. "What?"

He held a hand up to cup my face. "Keep going, please."

I sucked in my bottom lip and bit down. I had a habit of doing that when I was nervous. After the past year and a half, I had nearly chewed a hole right through it. He suddenly reached up and rested his index finger on my lip. It felt rough and I really wanted to open my mouth and see what it tasted like.

"Please don't bite that lip until you are ready to endure the consequences. I can't control myself when you do that."

"Really? I don't always even know I'm doing it."

"Yeah, well, you do it a lot."

"Huh, how about that? I didn't know. That would explain the tiny punctures inside my lip."

"You're doing it again."

I quickly released my lip from the insidious grasp of my tooth and decided to get the story done so we could finally move on to a happier ending.

"Well, so, I followed him to the party he was going to. I parked my car and debated about trying to go inside. In my deep subconscious, I knew I was sealing my fate, but part of me just wanted to hurry along the inevitable."

"And what was that?"

"That he would one day try to kill me."

"Jesus Christ, Frankie. Please don't tell me that's where this is headed."

Since I had pledged to be completely honest with him, I took the silent route on that one and forged ahead. "I got out of my car and silently walked up the drive, careful to stay to the shadows at the edge. When we got close to the door, I stalled, pretending I was looking for something in my purse. After a few minutes, I cautiously approached the door, surprised to find no one manning it. He had told me he was off to a political affair, which usually had a guest list heavily guarded. I crossed the threshold, and I immediately knew I was in trouble. It wasn't a hugely crowded affair. Either most people were going to be late, or there wasn't going to be enough people to give me good cover. I frantically searched for a place to hide out while planning my escape and crossed my fingers that down the hall to my right, had some unoccupied bedrooms. I ducked into the second door, and quietly turned to close it. When I turned back to face the room, I froze." Breathing in, breathing out, Frankie. "On the bed, was Patrick, except, he wasn't wearing anything I would ever expect. And he wasn't alone. He was one of three men surrounding a woman, who was tied to the bed and they were all over her and each other."

I wasn't sure I could get through much more, so grabbed the beer and downed it for all it was worth "What did he do?" He sounded super calm. Like waaay too calm. "He didn't do anything. He never did in public. But one surprised, angry eye was all the incentive I needed to get the fuck out of there. As fast as I could."

"I turned and ran to the front door and risked a glance back. The sick bastard wasn't even chasing me. I quietly slipped out the front door and ran like crazy to my car and drove home in record time. My heart rate was erratic, my pulse soaring and I knew I had one mission. Get out safely. But first, I needed to pack a few things. Stupid, I know. But there were some special things of mine I just couldn't leave behind. Ultimately, that was my hugest mistake."

"I raced into our bedroom and began to pile stuff into a small bag in our closet. I grabbed my mother's jewelry, my grandmother's necklace and the ultrasound I had gotten that morning."

"Fuck. Please baby, please don't go on."

"I had just confirmed I was five months pregnant that morning. I had suspected it for a while, but you can understand why I was apprehensive to confirm it. Before I decided whether to tell him or not, I needed to know if he was cheating on me. That was the whole impetus behind my following him. I had a life growing inside of me. I wasn't going to bring it into my world of abuse. It was the sign I needed that woke me up, finally.

"Please. You don't have to keep going." He grabbed me and tucked me as close as he could, but I continued on, as if in a trance.

"I was in the walk in closet when I heard him pull up. I turned out the light, opened my cell and dialled 911. My only chance was the police getting there before he went too far. I connected with the 911 operator and silently whispered my location and that my boyfriend was attacking me. I muted her and prayed she would send someone without continuing our conversation."

"I flattened myself against the wall, as close to the door as I could. I couldn't let him trap me in there. I heard him bellowing for me as he ran inside and slammed the front door. He was saying awful things and I knew without a doubt, getting out of the house tonight was imperative, but highly unlikely. I could hear him opening and closing doors, walking across the wood floors and then, as his voice grew louder, I knew he had come into the bedroom. I unmuted the cell so the dispatch agent could hear him and held my breath while I waited for him to check the closet."

"He was calling me every name in the book, filthy and angry names. I was used to hearing it, but it still shook me. If he was tossing all his eggs into the hatred basket, I was in for a huge beat down. I was jittery and positive he could hear me. In order to get out of there alive, I needed the police to time it just right. I needed to get out of there in one piece, but I also would love some good, hard evidence of his horrific abuse."

"He finally got to the closet and stepped inside. I knew my only shot was to run the instant his feet were past me and that's exactly what I did. I grabbed my cell and the bag, and bolted out behind him towards the front of the house. I shoved at him, taking him by surprise and he spun, disoriented for a moment. It was long enough to get some distance but he was no match for me. As I crossed the threshold from the bedroom into the hallway, he grabbed onto me."

"I tried to shake him loose, but he backhanded me and followed it with a vicious shove towards the stairs."

"Frankie, please stop. Please," Hardy begged me, but I was gone. I was on autopilot and just couldn't stop.

"I stumbled from the push and tripped and fell off balance. Only one thing mattered to me then. My baby. I screamed for him to stop, told him I didn't mean to hurt him, just that I was curious, but he was in a blind rage. Swinging at me and not hearing a word I was saying. He grabbed my arm and squeezed and I cried out in agony as my cell clattered to the floor. He saw it was connected and crushed it beneath his feet and kicked it down the staircase. He called me a fucking whore and punched me in the face until I dropped to my knees. It was then, as if in slow motion, I could see his next move was going to hit me right where I knew it would hurt the most. He pulled his foot back and slammed it into my stomach, four or five times, each time moving me closer to the staircase."

I felt wetness drop down from above and knew Hardy was crying. Strangely enough, I had no tears. I lifted my head and turned up to his sweet, loving face, soaked with tears that I couldn't shed anymore. I lifted my hand to swipe away his tears and reached my mouth up to his. He seemed to understand what I needed. I needed to feel the good, before I finished my story of evil. He connected his lips with mine and my mouth opened to pull all I could from him. He cradled my face in his hands and gave me all his goodness.

I reluctantly pulled away, knowing we couldn't get further until I finished the last and worst part of the story of my life.

"Eventually, I gave up the fight and he kicked me hard enough that I plummeted down the staircase. Fourteen stairs. Strangely enough, I counted on the way down and haven't ever forgotten. Hard, California tiled stairs. The next parts are fuzzy, but the girls filled in the blank spots for me when I woke up."

"I lost consciousness when I stopped rolling and that was when the police finally entered. They had heard the entire altercation, up until he crushed my phone. They arrested him on the spot and an ambulance took me to the nearest hospital. I was unconscious for nearly two days. I had a severe concussion, a broken arm, broken leg and internal organ damage. Oh, and I was hemorrhaging from my uterus. My baby. A little girl. Twenty-two weeks along in her tiny, short life."

My voice had taken on a ghost like quality. I heard myself as if listening from afar, but I couldn't seem to stop talking. "Ten toes, and ten little fingers. She was small for her gestation and I had irregular periods and so I hadn't known until eighteen weeks that I was pregnant. I kept it from him and so hadn't seen a doctor yet. He always seemed to know where I was at all times, so heading to an OB/GYN would have given away our situation. I didn't know whether he would want to keep her or not, but I knew that I couldn't raise her with him. Something in me understood that even though I refused to leave him."

"I named her Hannah. I held her before they took her to prepare for her burial. She was perfect. Tiny, a puff of blonde hair covering her head, long upper body and arms and short little legs, just like me. The nurses kept her from him. They kept my secret. She may have had him as a genetic donor, but he was no father. What father could do such horrific things to her mother? Even if he didn't know she existed, I feel like that knowledge wouldn't have stopped him."

"Of course, he came to see me, as did my parents. They all tried to push my "accident" under the rug, asking me how I could be so very clumsy. My own mother tried to get me to admit it was my fault. I was going to tell her I was pregnant, but decided after that parental advice, there was no way she was going to get any part of Hannah. The police came and they tried to get me to press charges. There was overwhelming evidence against him, but I just nodded politely, thanked them for coming and took control of the situation the best way I knew how. He would win. He had the power, the money and the influence. But I had Sam and George and George's husband, Finn. Between us and my nursing staff, we managed to pull off a stealth exit from the hospital. I said goodbye to Hannah, and trusted her funeral arrangements to George and Finn and Sam and I took off into the night."

"Jesus. All alone."

"Don't, Hardy. Don't feel sorry for me. I did it. I finally left him. I got out and that's something for me to be proud of. I moved around quite a bit at first and George kept tabs on him from her home base in LA. Eventually, his drive to find me and punish me started to wane. He had a huge sympathy campaign going on to find his missing girlfriend. The love of his life. The one he was going to marry. Soon after his campaign started, it stopped being useful to his career and he appeared to give up. However, I know, he still hasn't given up. And that's the whole point to this story Hardy. There are some things we need to discuss before this relationship goes any farther.

Chapter 25

Frankie

"OK, so that was pretty damn awful. What else do we need to discuss other than the next time I run into this dick, I can't be held responsible for what will happen."

"No, see that's just it. I'm purposefully not telling you his name so you can't run off and try to defend my honour."
"Oh, that's not all I'll be trying to do sweetheart. He deserves jail time. He's an abuser of women and that's just not ok with me."

I turned myself so I was facing him, hoping he would recognize the desperation that was written on my face. I grabbed a hold of his forearms and held on. "Hardy, please. I know he's all those things, but for me, please don't push this issue. I can't have more people hurt because I was a coward. Never again."
"Hey," he softened his hold on my arms. "You're not a coward. Not now, not then when you couldn't leave him. Just, stop. Please."

"No, I won't ever stop running. That's what I need to tell you. I move every few months, just to stay one step ahead of him. Whatever this is between us," I waved my arm between us. "It can't be anything more than a thing. I'm leaving in two weeks, Hardy. Weird things have been happening to me around here and I could swear I feel him here. I've started to make arrangements. I don't have much time left here."

"So, that's it. You've just decided for the both of us how it's going to go?"

"Hardy-"

He held his hands up in front of his face. "No, I don't want to hear your reasons. I understand them and they are good reasons, Frankie. But this is you and me. Not him and you. I'm not going to hurt you and I won't let him hurt you either."

"You can't guarantee that Hardy. He always comes out on top. He's freakin' Houdini when it comes to his ability to get out of tight situations."

He got up and put some more wood on the fire. Telling him it couldn't amount to anything, right on the night when it was amounting to so much more than something, hurt like I hadn't known it would. He had given me his back and I wasn't sure that I was going to get him to turn around again. So, I did the only thing I could, I went to him.

I got up and walked over to him and crouched down behind him, mirroring his stance. I laid my head and the front of my body down over his back and wrapped my arms around him. "Please, Hardy." My voice had become a whisper out of fear that I would startle him back to wanting to convince me of a new plan. There was no room for a new plan. There was only these next couple of weeks. He had to understand.

We stayed in that position for longer than my legs really wanted to. I felt him take in a deep breath and let it out as if he had come to some sort of conclusion. I eased myself off of his back and fell to the ground without much grace. I laid down and flopped my arms up above my head. I would surrender to his mood tonight. I needed him to understand where I was coming from but I also couldn't deny, I needed him. Period.

He sat down beside me and picked up my hand. He silently stared at it, seeming to be considering his next move. I laid beside him, unable to move a muscle. Surprising me, he tugged on my hand to pull me up. He didn't stop at a seated position, but yanked me all the way to standing. He pulled me behind him and moved us quickly down the hall, towards the bedrooms.

He pushed through the door to his bedroom and spun me around, trapping me between him and the wall. Something was going on. This wasn't my gentle, patient Hardy. He placed his hands on either side of my head, against the wall and pressed in close.

"Hardy, you're scaring me."

"Isn't this what you want, Red?" Shit, he only used his nickname for me lately when he was pissed. "You want to fuck me for a bit, have some fun, then move on?"

"What? Hardy, no! What's wrong with you?"

"What's wrong with me? Babe, you just told me of one of the most horrific stories. Only it wasn't a story, it was your life. It tore me to pieces inside. It took courage, it took bravery beyond what my men show up to work with some days, for you to give me that, to even, I don't know, be here with me. But, all you really needed was to get it off your chest, so you could feel better about getting me into bed and then leaving me."

Tears were falling that I was helpless to stop. "No, Hardy, stop this, please. You're twisting my intentions all around."

He lowered his face another fraction of an inch. We were practically nose to nose and I could feel the hurt and anger jumping off his skin, into my soul. "Am I? Isn't that exactly what you want?"

"It's for your own good. You don't want to be mixed up with me." I couldn't see him clearly anymore. My tears were blurring my vision and my heart was racing. My plan was totally fucked six ways to Sunday. How could this be happening? How could this have backfired so badly? "Hardy, please, can't you see? I don't want you to get hurt? He's evil. I have to leave here, I can't risk you getting destroyed by him. He will destroy you, make no mistake. He stops at nothing to get what he wants." I sucked in a sob when I saw the anguish and pain in his eyes.

He rested his forehead against mine and slowly moved his hands to frame my face. He raised his head so he was looking into my eyes. "A few days, or a week or so isn't enough for me, Frankie. I don't do casual. I might be the only guy in the world turning down a woman who is asking me to sleep with her with no expectations of a long term relationship, but I guess that's what I'm doing. You see, a couple of days ago, when I came to you and bared my soul and you took me in and pushed your fears aside and just held me, I fell in love with you. And fuck me, I didn't want to. After Sarah, I wasn't looking to love anyone ever again, but damned if it didn't start to happen the day you tripped over my dog. And so, no, I'm not ok with this just being a thing between us. I can't do that and survive the fall out."

And after he delivered the blow that hurt more than any physical hit could ever hurt, he dropped his hands, pushed back from me and walked away. "Get your things. I'll take you home."

Chapter 26

Frankie

The ride home was painful and I chose silence instead of begging him to listen and understand me. Not to mention how in the hell we had come to this emotional point. He loved me? How could he love me? In my world, people only pretended to love each other. He didn't really know what he was talking about. He loved the idea of me. No one can fall in love that quickly. We had only known each other for like, a little over a month.

We pulled into my driveway and I felt all my emotions come to a boiling point. This had to be goodbye. It was time to move on and it was time to accept Hardy wasn't going to be a part of what time I had left here. My heart was breaking and I was lost in a world of turmoil, when he threw open my door and reached in and grabbed me around my waist.

Being as tall as he was, he could easily wrap his arms around my waist while standing on the ground. I heard his exhausted sigh and then, "Fuck it." Having no idea what he meant, I wasn't prepared for him to mirror my words and actions from earlier in the night. He pulled back from my waist, hopped up on the running board and molded his mouth to mine. Tugging and aggressively attacking my lips like he was saying goodbye with this kiss.

He wrapped his arms around me, holding me steady behind my neck, while he pulled my bottom lip down with his teeth. I opened my mouth and his tongue took control and deepened the kiss. We stayed in this dance, both of us jockeying for position. I had never in my life been kissed with such passion, with such desire with such love.

"Inside." He broke free to mutter that one word. The one word that had me so confused.

"Hardy, wait."

"No, no more waiting. Inside." He hopped down from the truck and grabbed my waist on his way by, effectively making this decision for me. He pulled me aside, slammed the door and grabbed my keys to unlock the door. Making quick work of my lock, he swung open the door, grabbed my hand and took me inside, shutting the door behind me.

"Bedroom. Now."

Ok, his caveman act was starting to piss me off and I had a serious case of whiplash. I dug my proverbial heel in and jerked my hand out of his clutches. "Hardy!" I yelled. "What the hell is going on with you?"

He backed up and grabbed my hand and spun me around, up against the wall. "I thought I could do it, Red. I thought I could walk away but if you're only giving me a week or two, I'm in."

Wow, oh wow. I didn't have time to think about it. He caged me in against the wall and kissed me like we may never have another moment together. It was hard, it was fast but it was loving and oh shit, who was I kidding? It was amazing.

He left my mouth and began to explore the side of my neck, trailing his lips down, stopping to nibble on the sensitive bits behind and around my ear. "Hi," he whispered against my ear.

I smiled and turned my head to look at him. He was grinning, dimples out. "Hi," I whispered back.

"Are you good, babe?"

"Yeah." It was about all I could get out. This man. We met by accident but it was like he was my gift at the end of journey filled with horror. I made it through and now I get him. But I couldn't keep him. It was a gift with an expiration date. I pushed that thought quickly aside as he got back to his mission of kissing me all over. His free hand had started stroking me, drawing beautiful circles around my side and down my leg, until it reached the hem of my dress, where it ducked under and began to retrace its path, this time, skin on skin.

He kissed a path down and across my neck, over to offer the same treatment to the other side. My hands were flattened against the wall, only in order to hold me up. My knees were going to give out at any time. I thought being with Hardy this way was going to help me. Help me get over Patrick, help me have some fun for once, but never did I ever imagine, it would be like this. I had my palms flattened to the wall to save myself. If I released them from the wall, I had no idea how I would stay standing.

I had never felt such immense attraction and electricity with a man before. I had always thought Hardy was hot, and kind and sweet and amazing, but this was a whole new level of Hardy Hanson. Hardy 2.0. I longed to get under his shirt and confirm my darkest suspicions. Confirm that he was hard all over, starting with washboard abs, biceps I could hang off of and of course, I already knew he was hard in one specific location. That hardness was currently pulsing against me and it's the main reason I was in the state I was in.

Hardy made it back to my mouth and I welcomed him inside. His kisses sent shivers down my body right down to the place it counted the most. His hand that had journeyed under my dress was now making its way under my panties and around my back to grip my rear and thankfully, hold me steady. He lifted me up and I held onto him with my legs as he walked un into my bedroom.

We never broke contact with each other and soon, I felt the edge of my bed against the back of my legs. He let go of my ass, in order to slowly support us as we laid down on the bed. I was lying on my back and Hardy was stretched out over top of me, supporting himself on his arms so as not to crush me.

"Babe, are you ok? Just once this moves to the next level, I don't know how easy it will for me to stop."

I reached up to swipe some hair off his forehead and gently moved to cup his cheek. "Don't. Please. Just forget about my past and show me today. Show me what it's really supposed to feel like. Please, Hardy. Erase my past."

"Ah, Red. I don't know if I can forget your past. I'm freaking out a bit here. I've wanted inside you for so long, that I am positive, had you not told me your story, this here would have been over in nearly a minute. But, you did tell me and I couldn't stand myself if I hurt you or rushed through this."

"There's no rule saying we can only do this once, Hardy. I need you, fast. Then slow. Now."

I watched him struggle for all of two seconds before he lunged at me and proceeded to kiss me everywhere. His mouth lit me on fire, igniting something in me that had long since burned out. I was alive and nothing was going to stop me from living tonight. Not Patrick, not Hardy and not my stupid brain.

He rolled my loose top up and eased a breast out from my bra and began to circle the nipple with his tongue pulling it into his mouth as far as he could. I heard a soft moaning sound and wondered how Hardy had change his tone so quickly. When I heard it a second time, I suddenly realized it was coming from me. I didn't moan. I was mute during sex. What in the bloody hell was happening to me?

When he switched to the other side, freeing my right breast and paying as much attention, if not more to it, I gave into the urge to moan and gave it my all. I had always judged those that had loud sex and had banged on my fair share of hotel and bedroom walls in my day. But now I found myself making those obnoxious sounds and I didn't give a flying fuck who could hear.

That was it. I needed his shirt off, now. I reached down and grazed his abdomen and slid my hands down and under the hem of his shirt. I tugged it upwards, hopefully letting him know I needed it off within the next five seconds or there was no telling what I would do. He paused what he was doing and reared back to pull his shirt over his head and I realized my over-active imagination wasn't over-active after all. He did have the requisite six pack abs. He had smooth and rounded shoulders begging to be touched. His arms were all length and muscle and decidedly male. And then back to those abs. I trailed my fingers delicately over them and heard him abruptly intake a sharp breath. They flexed and moved beneath my touch, as if they were pulsing and pushing me in the direction they wanted me to move.

I obliged and felt my way over to the deep V that was cut into the sides of his body, lightly tracing it's path, downwards, where I finally arrived at my destination. Hardy grabbed a hold of my hand stopping it before it landed on its mark.

"Don't. Please. Not unless you want this to be over before it really gets started."

He took control of my hands and lifted them up and above my head with one hand and slowly pulling my top upwards with his other hand. I sat up and he pulled the shirt up and over my head, never once breaking eye contact with me.

He held me up with a hand on my back while unfastening my bra and helping me slide it down and off my arms. I was now nearly naked and unsure of myself. The last time I had been naked with a man, he had told me I could stand to lose a few pounds. Of course, he was so self-involved, he didn't notice that those few pounds were located precisely in the area of my expanding uterus.

Hardy gently set me back down and kicked off his boots, pulled down his socks and much to my surprise and delight, dropped his pants. He stretched himself back over me and just stared at me for a minute.

"We really gonna do this, Red?"

I answered him with a kiss and then it was on. We wrestled with control. It was like a switch had been flipped inside of me. Not since college had I been so turned on by a man. I eventually gave into the sensations and let him set the pace and take over. He had me pinned down beneath him, but he still floated above me, never once settling his weight on top of me. I wanted to tell him not to be afraid of hurting me, but it was beyond my abilities to create anything that constituted a real word at this point in time.

He slipped a hand inside my panties and then proceeded to send racing beams of fire inside of me with his finger. I arched off the bed and gave up on my moaning issue right then and there. I let go like I had never done before. I was safe and loved and damn but I needed this man inside of me.

"Jesus, babe. I had no idea. No fuckin' clue." He was muttering to himself like a lunatic but I didn't care. It had been a long time since someone had treated me with this kind of care. "Thank God I changed my mind on the drive over here." He increased his speed while I searched for the release that was building inside of me.

"Stop talking, Hardy."

I could feel his smile against my skin. "You got it."

His thumb finally decided to put me out of my misery and found the spot that could make it all better and began slow, circular motions that would guarantee a happy ending for me. I moved my hips in a restless movement, trying to get him to go harder, move faster. He took the hint and picked up his pace while drawing a nipple into his mouth and pulling with all his gentle might.

I came with everything I had been holding in all those years. After all the years of abuse and all the years of feeling like I was less than the woman I now know myself to be, I burst into tears, again. Just the greatest way to say to the man you're with, that was the most amazing thing I had experienced in a long time. Yup, so cool.

"I'm sorry." Shit, now they were getting worse. What in the hell was happening to me?

"Frankie, hush baby. Let it out." He wrapped me up in his arms and pulled the duvet up around us. We were safe inside this tiny cocoon he had made. But still, the damn tears wouldn't stop. They were erupting inside of me and spilling out of every available exit. I was dripping snot and tears and most likely drool too. I had completely lost my mind.

"Sorry." I said between sobs and hiccups and sniffles. "I'm not sure what's happening."

"I am. It's happened to me before. And don't take this the wrong way, I was so embarrassed. It happened the first time I, ah, well never mind. Just trust me. It's your time to let go in all ways. Don't worry about me. Out of all the people in the world, I'm happy it was with me." He pressed a soft kiss to my temple and continued to rock and shush me until my tears finally stopped.

"Thank-you. I just can't believe that happened. You say it's ok, but you must be looking for a quick point of exit. We haven't even gotten to the good part yet and I'm already a mess."

"That part can wait."

I looked up at him and those damn gorgeous brown eyes. "That's not fair to you, Hardy. Just give me a minute to calm down and then we can start over."

"Shit, Red. What kind of man do you think I am? There's no way we're moving any further today than we already have. It's late and you're tired and emotionally exhausted. Besides, tonight has been one of the craziest nights of my life. I'm not sure my performance would have been as mind blowing as you would be expecting."

I barked out a laugh. "I think even at your worst, you would have been perfect."

"Well, now you're just being kind. You're killing me with that, Frankie. A man can only take so much kindness. No fuckin' way I'm going soft." He rolled me underneath him and stretched out on top again. "Seriously, let's just get some sleep. I've got to work early and you have to do whatever it is you do all day." He smirked and I gave him my best stink eye.

"Meet me for a run tomorrow?"

"I wouldn't be any other place. I leave work most days at the same time to grab Chuck and go for a run. I just switched it to earlier in the day before we met and wouldn't you know that on that particular day, I run west, but Chuck decided to take off at light speed east and run head first into you. If I didn't know better, I would think he kinda chose you."

I laughed, wiped away the last of my tears and sent a silent thanks to the universe for that. I didn't know how much longer I had with Hardy, but I was determined to make the most of it. The problem was, he said he loved me. There was no way this was going to end well for us.

"Penny for your thoughts?"

Damn, my stupid open book facial expressions screwed me again. "Just wondering where you came from. After all that I told you tonight, you're still here. In my bed, making me feel comfortable, safe and relaxed like I haven't felt, well, probably ever."

"I'll pretend that explanation is what you were really thinking about due to exhaustion." He planted a chaste, quick kiss on my lips and rolled off to the side. He swung his arm around my waist and pulled me into his chest, my back to his front.

"Mmmm," he just mumbled into my hair. I wasn't sure what to do or if I could sleep. I waited for a while until his breathing evened out and slipped out of his embrace and out into my darkened living room.

I sat on the couch and stared into the black ocean with only the moonlight streaming around the swirling waves. What was I going to do with the man asleep in my bed? If only we had met a few years ago, things would be different. I couldn't stay here much longer. I didn't want to hurt him but damn, I had to keep protecting myself. I would never again let my safety leave my hands.

I noticed a flash of movement outside and was glad that I had chosen not to turn on any lights. In my haste to get a taste of Hardy, I hadn't seen to my usual lock up routine. Shit, things were already going bad and we hadn't even slept together yet. I usually pulled the shutters on the back windows, checked all the locks and made sure all the blinds were drawn around the house. I moved to get up and do just that when I saw the flash of movement again. It was close to the water's edge.

Curious, I got up to investigate. I slowly drew the shutters closed across the left side of the back window, then the right. Whatever it was, it was still down there. The moonlight was glinting off something in the air, like it was being held by someone. It was too dark for me to make out. I slowly pulled one shutter rung open to try out my spying skills, when suddenly, a pair of arms grabbed me from behind.

I screamed and twisted around to try to run, when a slow kiss was planted on my neck from behind. "Looking for something?"

"Hardy! Shit. You scared me!" My breathing slowly returned to normal but my brain was all over the place.

"Sorry, babe. I thought you heard me. You must have been totally focused on whatever you were looking at."

I frowned. I had lost my edge. It was official. I needed to start to get my ass to the next location. I was getting too comfortable here and wasn't paying attention. First, I didn't lock up, then I missed Hardy not trying to sneak up on me. A few months ago, that never would have ever happened.

"What's going on in that head of yours? Stop, stop overthinking this and let it be. Let us be. Even if it's just until your two week expiration date. But know this, I plan on busting through that expiration date. I've been given a second chance and sure as shit, I'm not going to let you go without proving to you I can keep you safe and happy and loved."

I reached my hand up to cup his cheek. "Oh sweetheart, my brave, amazing man. Can't you see? He'll never stop. I'll never stop being afraid and we can never be an us. Only for this short period of time, so, you're right. Let's go back to bed and be together and enjoy what we have now, 'cause we both know that it's a gift."

He grabbed a hold of my wrist and I saw a sadness in his deep brown eyes. "Don't. Just stop. Please." He took my hand and led me down the hall to the bedroom, laid me down, tucked me in, scooted in behind me and we drifted off together.

Chapter 27

Frankie

I woke the next day to an empty bed, with a note on the pillow.

Morning, babe. Gone to work. Meet you here at 10 for a run. Miss you already,

H

I smiled and rolled over to get my day started. It was seven o'clock and I had a lot of work to get started on before Hardy got here for our run.

I quickly showered and dressed in my gear and then sat down at my laptop and got to work on the research I needed to do in order to find a new place to live. I was going to miss the ocean, but I thought perhaps something in the mountains would work this time around. I obviously needed to get even more isolated that this place. A remote cabin should do the trick.

Before I knew it, a knock sounded at the door. I slammed the laptop shut and ran to answer it. What I saw on the other side took my breath away. He was wearing a sleeveless shirt, paired with long running shorts and his hair was flopping around in the strong ocean breeze.

He was leaning sexily against my door frame grinning like a little boy. I couldn't help but smile in spite of myself. "Hey gorgeous," he said. "Feel like getting your ass kicked in a race?"

"Hah, you wish. You're all fast at the start, then your staying power fizzles at the end."

"Are you trying to trash talk me? Oh, you're so dead." He lunged for me and picked me up by the waist and threw me over his shoulder. Luckily, I was ready for our run and formulated a plan as he raced with me in his expert fireman's hold towards the water. Still, my genius plan didn't stop me from squealing like a school girl. "Put me down, Hardy!"

"Not until I'm good and ready, Little Red. This fireman can run for days with a little thing like you thrown over his shoulder."

Belatedly, I realized this could be true. Still I let him think he was going to win this battle and went slack and started to implement my plan. "Hardy, please, stop, you're going to make me throw up. I can't be upside down. I have a condition." He started to slow. Almost there. Almost to the point I wanted to get him to.

"What kind of condition?"

I was about to spit out some made up condition, when I realized being a fireman, and trained in emergency situations, he might have a knowledge of most medical conditions, and if not, still could recognize a bull shitter from a mile away, let alone, one he had upside down, slung over his back, whose face was up front and personal with his beautifully sculpted rear end.

It didn't matter. We were in the position. "Upsidedownitis."

"That the best you can do?"

"Nope, not even close." I took advantage of his relaxed position to reach down to the sand and at the same time, swing my legs over his shoulders, performing a hand stand of sorts. I leaped up and charged him, pushing him backwards, right into the next huge wave crashing in. He was down and out and completely soaked.

I spent the next minute jumping up and down in glee, yelling and whooping my victory chants and running around in circles. Hardy just sat there, completely drenched and smiled his full on dimpled grin at me. I scooted over to him, staying just out of his reach. "Take that, Hardy Hanson, alpha male, firefighter extraordinaire. You just got bested by teeny, tiny little 'ole me."

"Ok. You win. Is that what you wanted to hear? You beat me, fair and square, but know this. It's on, like fucking donkey kong. Can you please help me up?" He reached out his hand and I leaned forward to grab and help him up. Too late, I looked into his eyes and saw that sneaky gleam as he yanked me forward, off balance, where I landed right on top of him. In the ocean. Drenched and laughing harder than I had in oh so long.

"You snake. That was evil."

"Ok, Upsidedownitis. We're even," he paused. "For now."

A wave chose that moment to crash in on us and we both flew to the shore, sputtering and laughing our heads off, limbs completely tangled up. We ended up side by side, face to face. Hardy lunged in and effectively stopped my laughing with a hard, challenging kiss. I accepted that challenge and gave him as good as he was giving, tugging on his lower lip, drawing it deep into my mouth.

He wrapped his arm around me, pulling me closer him and trapping me to his chest. He took the kiss deeper and I could feel how turned on he was and I couldn't help but feel a little bit sorry for him. He probably was going to go back to work with a bad case of blue balls as we hardly had time or the ability to finish this session properly.

"Little Red, what the hell happened to our run?"

He pulled back from the kiss with great effort, eyes closed, breathing deeply. "What are you doing later?"

"The usual."

"Want to do the usual with me? I'm on call tonight, but we could eat in? Then watch a movie?"

"I don't have a t.v."

He pulled back with an exaggerated look of surprise on his face. "What the hell, Red? That is messed up. How do you watch sports and stuff?"

"I don't?"

He looked pensive and then broke into a smile. "Well then, you'll just have to come hang out at my place tonight and I will educate you on the finer points of baseball. Then, you can pick out a movie of your liking."

"Is that so?"

"It is." And I guess that was that. "So, as much as I have pictured lying on the beach with you, in my mind, we weren't wearing quite so many pieces of clothing and there wasn't sand stuck in every God forsaken place on my body. I'm going to need to borrow your shower and your dryer in order to make it back to work without looking like a drowned rat."

He hopped up and held out his hand to me. I eyed it skeptically, but took it anyway. He pulled me to standing, crowding me in so our bodies rubbed up against each other. He smiled his mischievous grin, waggled his eyebrows and grabbed my hand while turning to head back to my house.

"Does your team know about me?"

"Kind of."

"Kind of?"

"Well, they obviously know you exist, as you met a couple of them the other night at the bar and the BBQ, but they don't know the extent of our relationship. They don't know we run every day together and they have no clue we've had a sleepover."

I giggled. Then covered my mouth with my hand. What the hell was wrong with me? I don't giggle. He looked back at me over his shoulder and grinned and squeezed my hand and led me home.

Hardy stripped down and hopped into the shower, leaving his wet clothes for me to put into the dryer. I was busy taking off my offensive, squeaking wet shoes when had stripped down and happened to chance a look up to see that sculpted ass disappear into my bathroom. I heaved a huge sigh and smiled in spite of my reservations at getting too close to him. He was just too damn amazing and adorable and hot and sexy. I mean really, a firefighter, so cliché.

I peeled off my socks and wet clothes and grabbed some fresh shorts and a t-shirt and threw our wet clothes into the dryer and took a minute to really question what it was I was doing here. I knew Hardy was all in and for some reason, had decided to not protect his heart. I was going to hurt him and the thought of that made me sick to my stomach. There was something happening between us, and I couldn't, or most likely, didn't want to define it, but it was something strong and I was slowly losing my will to resist it.

As I was thinking all this through, leaning up against my bedroom door frame, out steps Hardy Hanson. Naked as the day he was born, but certainly all grown up. Wrapping a towel around his key parts, knowing full well what he was doing. He was going to fight dirty. I had it all up close and personal last night, but that was last night. In the dark. With my eyes closed. This was in glorious bright lights with a super massive 3D effect, if you know what I mean.

He clearly worked hard at keeping his body fit. Not an ounce of fat on it. He had strong, sculpted arms, clearly defined, but not too big pecs and abs that you could play with for hours. I could make out a few tattoos in the light of day. Looked like the traditional fireman decoration, but there was another in the area of his heart. It looked like script so I would need to get a closer look to see exactly what it was. Of course, that was my excuse for crossing the room. I needed to see his tattoo.

"Can I help you with something?"

I smiled and tried my hardest to look sexy. It couldn't have worked. He began to look scared. I must have blown right by sexy and went to crazed stalker. I stopped right in front of him and reached out to catch a few stray drips of water that had escaped his towel. He grabbed my hand before I could reach my destination. "Now, now. I've got to get to work and that's not going to happen if I let you touch me. Save that fun for later." He smirked, cocky bastard, and walked past me and out into the hallway to find his clothes.

"Look, Hardy-"

"Nope, got to get to work. I can tell you're gearing up to rehash last night's conversation and I get it. You're leaving soon, et cetera, et cetera. So you say." He bent over to push on his squishy shoes, grimaced and decided against it. "Fuck, my shoes are a mess. I'm going to have to go back barefoot. That should go over well." He looked up at me. I was still standing in the middle of my room, eyes closed and fists clenched.

I felt him come up in front of me, yet still, wasn't going to open my eyes. He rested his forehead on mine and grabbed a hold of my hands in his. "Babe, don't be afraid of this. Ok? I'm not going to hurt you."

"I know Hardy," I whispered. "I'm going to hurt you."

I opened my glistening eyes to the man that could bring down all my carefully erected perimeters. A single tear ran down my face and he caught it with his index finger. "You let me worry about my heart. Let me protect you, Frankie. I can do that for us. I'd given up on ever finding another woman I wanted to be with more than I wanted to be alone. Then Chuck ran you over and now I've got you. I'm not letting you go without a fight, you can count on that."

He leaned over and placed the sweetest kiss on my lips, tucked my hair behind my ears and turned and walked to his truck. I sunk to the floor and rested my back against my bed willing myself to freak out and start to cry, but instead, I had the hugest, goofiest grin on my face.

I may not be sticking around much longer, but while I was here, I had the love of this amazing man and I was going to enjoy him as much as I could.

Chapter 28

Hardy

I walked back into the station, barefoot and fancy free.

"Hey Chief. Forget something?" Will was walking out of my office as I was trying to get in. I just smiled and shifted to get by him. My private life was just that, private, but Will was my best friend and knew all the shit that went with being with me. I knew he wasn't going to give up.

"Nope, just went for a run."

"In the ocean? You're wet and by the way, not wearing any shoes."

"Observant."

"Shit, what the hell, Hardy? You going to share?"

I went into my locker and got my uniform out, reached around him and closed my door and pulled the shade on the door window. "I went for a run, with Frankie, in the ocean. We didn't get very far. We got pretty wet. End of story."

I stripped off my clothes and gave him my ass while I got dressed again.

"Shit, my eyes. Cover that shit up lover boy." He howled, then dropped down into a chair. "So, this gonna end badly?"

"Possibly. No, more like probably."

"Then I gotta ask, why?"

I turned around, nearly done. "Because she's my second chance. I'm in Will. She just doesn't know it yet. There's a ton of crap that comes along with her, but I don't care. I'm in."

Will whistled and barked out a laugh. "Well, I'll be damned. Finally. Well, I hope you've met your match in more ways than one, you stubborn ass." He lost his smile and turned serious. "I hope she doesn't wreck you, man, but I also gotta say, I'm happy for you."

"Thanks. Now, are you done? 'Cause sharing time is over."

"Yeah, yeah. I've got paperwork to get to. Later."

He left and I sat down and got back to work, finding it awfully hard to focus. I knew I was in for a fight, but it wasn't anything I was ready to back down from…..yet.

Chapter 29

Frankie

I couldn't focus on much the rest of the day so gave up and texted Sam as I knew George was busy with baby and Finn and rarely got a chance to talk. However, Sam was on set in Ireland and had loads of time.

> So, got some news.

Spill it.

> Good or bad news first?

For the love of Christ.

> Grouchy

You have no idea.

> Hardy says he loves me

WTF! When the hell did that happen?

> Last night

Oooo, last night?

> Yes, last night ;)

Winky face. I see. Isn't that a little fast?

> We've known each other for over a month.

Yeah, I guess. Whatcha gonna do? You don't do falling in love.

> Not sure. I think he's found me.

Jesus Christ. Fuck. What does Hardy think?

> He doesn't know.

Frances. What in the hell? You shouldn't be alone. Tell him or I will.

> I know. I'm handling it.

How do you know he's found you?

> Nothing concrete. Just weird coincidences. And weird strangers hanging around at odd times.

Hm. K. Please move in with lover boy.

    What! What happened to that's too fast?

Now I think it's too slow. Sue me. I'm in fucking Ireland, the capital of rain, fog and arrogant drunks and miserable men.

    Wanna talk?

Nope.

    K, gotta run.

Tell him…..or else….

    Scary you are

Thanks Yoda.

I had a stupid grin on my face. I didn't need a mirror to know it was stupid big, I just knew. I knew because for the first time, in possibly forever years, I was happy. But more incredible than that, I was allowing myself to feel happy. I was still insanely unsure about starting whatever it was we were starting, but I was willing, for the time being, to let myself just enjoy what Hardy did for me. Who knows, maybe after I left we could try the long distance thing. Maybe I didn't have to go too far away.

Excitedly, I opened my laptop to redo my search area. I narrowed my map to locations within a two to three hour drive from here and found all sorts of inland, remote options. I would have to really sit down and talk to Hardy about how this could work. I was nervous adding another person into the finite mix of people who knew how to find me. He would make the third. Sam, George, and now Hardy. This could work. I busied myself with the new task of finding my next home with that stupid grin still on my face.

A few hours passed and I had narrowed my search down to a handful of areas and a dozen houses that looked like they may work. I was excited to tell Hardy my new plan. But first, I was going for a run and then a shower, then get ready for our date tonight.

I grabbed my favourite running gear from the dryer and bent over to pick up my shoes. I noticed a piece of paper on the floor and reached to grab it so I could throw it out. I would be the first to admit that I had a bad case of OCD, and stray scraps of paper on the floor irritated me. Hardy must have dropped it on his way out this morning.

I was about to throw it in the garbage when I noticed it had some writing on it. I turned it over and saw a series of numbers written on it. They looked vaguely familiar, but I couldn't immediately place them. I decided to hold onto the paper and have a closer look when I came back from my run.

I wasn't looking forward to my run today. I knew there would be no Hardy meeting me at the half way point. I had come to rely on him to keep me focused and motivated while on the run. I took off, not giving much thought to anything other than one step at a time getting through this run.

My phone beeped, letting me know I had an incoming text. Damn, I swipe open the phone to see it's nearly seven and I am not close to being ready.

> Hey babe, leaving in five. Pack an overnight bag. ;)

I shook my head while laughing to myself. A winky face. He was so ahead of his time.

Drive slow. Standing here naked and not sure what to wear.

> Just stay as you are and you'll be perfectly dressed. Now speeding.

☺

I threw the phone down on the bed and put it in high gear. He was so not seeing me naked in the light of day. I am just not as impressive as his perfect body. I went over to my closet and grabbed an acceptable outfit, jeans and a t-shirt and cardigan, and as I was getting dressed, it hit me. Those numbers.

I sank down onto the floor, shaking and not sure what to do. The string of numbers was the code to disarming my alarm. I knew instantly that it was him. I didn't need to think or try to remember if I had written it down or gave it to Hardy. It was his handwriting and it was terrifying.

I ran from room to room, closing the blinds and double checking the doors and windows were locked. He had been inside my house. Jesus. I had run out of time, but I wasn't ready. I hadn't secured anything, I didn't know where to go or how to get there. Shit.

Think, Frances. Calm down and think.

I paced my bedroom and tried to think, but nothing would come together. My brain was so scattered. I knew staying this long was a mistake. Damn you Hardy Hanson. This was his fault, making me fall for him and start to believe we could be here together and never be found.

I knew what I had to do. I had to get out. I wouldn't lead him to Hardy and I wouldn't just sit around and wait for him to attack me. I needed to move while he still thought he had the upper hand.

I began to fly around my room, throwing stuff into my suitcase. I was so intent on getting packed and running that I didn't hear the door open. Belatedly, I realized I must not have locked it.

"I know I told you to pack for a sleepover, but don't you think that's a little too much?"

I whipped around and pulled in a quick breath. "Hardy."

"Last time I checked. Are you ok?"

I was staring. Damn, I needed to start acting normal and get rid of him just for a bit. Long enough for me to throw him off my trail. "Yes, fine. Just while I was packing, I thought I would put some of my stuff into storage. My closet was getting too full." God, he was hot. He was still in his uniform and what woman with a heartbeat could resist a man in a uniform? I needed to resist him if I knew what was good for both of us.

"Do you think it would be ok if I just met you at your house? I want to have my car there for tomorrow. Then I won't have to wake up as early as you to get a ride home."

"Yeah, sure, that sounds like a great idea. However, I was thinking, I could just give you a ride home, well, another day, like say, three or four days from now."

Dimples. Why did he have to be born with those dimples? And those adorable eyes, and that freaking hotter than hell body?

"Oh yeah? Three of four days, huh. That's awful presumptuous of you Mr. Hanson. Why don't we take it day by day?"

He narrowed his eyes and I started to sweat. "Why are you packing all your jewelry, and books and shit from your night stand and dresser?"
"I just thought I would de-clutter."

"Fuck." He ground out the curse word to the point I knew he had figured me out. He strode over to where I was standing and grabbed me by the shoulders. "You're leaving, aren't you?"

"It's best for-"

"Do not even try to spin that bullshit answer on me. It's not best for me, babe, and don't start telling me it is." He stormed over to my suitcase that was on my bed and halfway full and began pulling stuff out. I grabbed his arm and pulled him back to me.

"Hardy, please, stop. You knew this might happen. No, not might, was going to happen. I never lied to you."

"No, Red," he quietly said. "You never lied to me, but I thought we had decided to give it a try and see where it might lead us. I told you I loved you for God's sake." His voice cracked at the end and it nearly undid me.

"Please. Sweetheart, please understand." The tears started to flow and I reached out to grab him.

"You're either in or you're out, and I get your reasons, but I can't be the one always on our side. What's it gonna be?"

I stared at him. The silence spoke for me and it destroyed me. This kind, gentle, loving man didn't deserve this. He deserved a woman who could commit to him forever, and so, I said nothing.

And with that, he strode past me and out the door.

I stood there wondering what the hell had just happened, then promptly fell to the floor and cursed the day I met that asshole who would ruin my life. I cursed my parents for deciding my future was with him, and I cursed myself for falling in love with a man who could melt me just with a simple smile.

I sunk my head into my hands. Damn revelations. They always came too late. I loved him. Somehow, that sneaky bastard had gotten me to fall in love with him without me knowing it. Oh, he was good. But, was he right? Could he make this fear and paranoia go away? Could he single handedly save me?

Chapter 30

Frankie

Days went by, crawling at the speed of a turtle. I stopped running, stopped painting and just sat on my deck and stared the ocean down. I hadn't had any movement on the stalker front and hadn't heard a word from Hardy. Of course, I hadn't reached out to him either. I had royally messed this up.

On the fourth day since my epic screw up, I sat and watched the waves come in and move out again, clearing away all the sand and debris in their way. My heart hurt so badly and I felt like all the decisions and good intentions I had were slowly tearing me apart. I wiped away the stupid tears and tried to set my mind to thinking. "Stop thinking and start living, Frankie." Hardy had been saying that since the moment we met. I laughed out loud, finally willing to admit that maybe he was right and now it was probably too late. But I had to try. I was done letting Patrick's abuse define the rest of my life. I was done crying and I was so fucking done being scared.

I pulled myself up and continued the packing I had left on the floor. I needed the whole suitcase for this trip. I was going on a sleepover at Hardy's house and I wasn't coming back until we had figured out a plan, together. I was going to get him back and that was all I could focus on for this moment in time. One foot in front of the other, Frances. Get your bag packed, get in the car, drive to Hardy's, convince him to not be done with me. Those are the goals today, girl. Let's get started.

I threw my stuff into the trunk of the car and peeled out of my driveway, praying that Hardy was home and not out gallivanting somewhere. As I was driving, my phone rang, it was George. I hit accept, even though I truly had no idea what in the hell I was going to talk about that wouldn't start the damn tears again.

"Hey." I tried to make my voice sound super chipper.

"Hey yourself. I don't have long and you know I hate talking on the phone, but I wanted to give you a heads up. Are you ok to talk?"

"Just driving, but fine."

"You don't sound fine. I think this should probably wait until you aren't operating a motorized vehicle and don't sound like your dog done gone and died on you."

"I don't have a dog.
"Yeah, ok. That's the part of that statement you chose to focus on. What's going on, Franks?"

And then the fucking torrential tear storm came back with a vengeance and I couldn't see where the hell I was going. I knew I was getting close to his house but I hadn't been paying attention and now my tears were blocking my vision. I found a safe spot to pull over and threw the car in park.

"Frankie? What's going on?"

Unlike Sam, who would be screaming into the phone while booking a plane ticket out here while I cried, George was a patient listener. She always was great at sitting back and assessing situations and letting us rant and scream and then only butting in when asked to. I was so grateful she had somehow felt the spirit move her to call me.

My sobs finally quieted until it was just a little sniffle here and there. I could hear soft whispering in the background. "Are you with Finn?"

"Yeah, he's here, using my giant belly as his own personal pillow. Now, are you done? Can you tell me what caused that meltdown?"

"So much has happened in the past two days I don't even know where to begin. Hardy said he loves me, I think I might love him too, Patrick has been inside my house, Hardy broke up with me after he found me packing to steal away in the night without telling him, and now I'm on my way over to Hardy's to beg him to take me back and try to figure out a way to be rid of Patrick, once and for all."
"Holy shit on a stick, you're in love?"

"That's the part of the statement you chose to focus on?"

"Touché. But, come on, it's huge. But I don't want to keep you from your mission. However, I called to warn you about Patrick. I had only just heard he has been doubling his efforts to find you. Looks like he is going to run for the senate and has taken a liking to a new lucky lady. It's Serena Albright (check name), that skanky actress that tried to break Finn and I up ages ago."

I heard Finn yell in the background, "wasn't ever going to happen babe." I loved that man for how much he loved George. "Anyway, before I was so rudely interrupted," I heard her snicker and assumed Finn was trying to tickle her. It was his favourite way to torture her. "What I'm trying to say is that he's been asking around about you again and now I haven't seen or heard of him for days. But, I guess you may already have found him. What the fuck Frankie. You need to tell the police."

"I know, but I just don't think it will do any good. He has the police completely fooled."
She heard George sigh. "I know. Stupid bastard. Well, at least tell Hardy and see what he thinks."

"I don't want Hardy going all crazy and doing something he may live to regret, George."

"Frankie, if you love him and he loves you, you need to be open and honest with him. He's gonna want to know that this happened."

"Well, I've got to run. It's getting pretty dark here and I have only been to his place once and am not too sure where I'm going. Love you George. Kiss that belly and Finn for me." I quickly hung up before the lecture began in earnest and pulled back out onto the road.

At least George's phone call gave me some time to get my thoughts together. I now knew it would be bad to tell Hardy specifically why I was running. I would have to skirt around the fact Patrick had been in my home. I would tell him what George told me and I would just have to let what happened, happen. I knew if he knew Patrick was around, he would go ballistic and do something he would later regret and I wasn't about to let that happen to him.

I finally pulled into his driveway and parked. His truck wasn't there, which most likely meant he wasn't home. Well, I would just have to wait him out.

I settled in for who knew how long and began to debate my hasty plan when the sun was fully set and there was no sign of Hardy. I had run out of games to play and people to text, especially since I only had a handful of people on my phone, and I was getting antsy. Where in the hell was he? What if he had gotten called out to a fire? Who knew how long he would be gone for.

I couldn't go back to my house. It was too dangerous now. I wished like hell I had asked Hardy if he kept a spare key outside somewhere. I wasn't sure he would be happy to see me inside his house, but I would have felt a hell of a lot safer inside than out here in my car.

I reclined my seat and grabbed a throw that was doubling as a seat cover in the back and decided to try to get some sleep, hidden down in the seat, so no one could see I was here. I soon drifted off to sleep and missed the cab pulling up alongside my car an hour or so later. What I couldn't have missed was the loud bang on my window, which made me jump a mile and scream for my life.

"What are you doin' here, Frankie?"

Oh, shit. He didn't sound super happy to see me. Why did I race over here before thinking? I knew I should have just up and left.

"I came to see you." God, this was stupid. We were having a conversation through the window. I gathered my purse and phone and opened the door to hop out and instead sent Hardy stumbling backwards. The jerk was stone cold drunk. Jesus.

"Hardy, have you been out drinking? Aren't you on call tonight?"

"Yup. Annnnd, yup. I mean nope. They pulled me off call this week." He forged his way towards the door and I wondered, not for the first time tonight, what in the hell I was doing.

He swayed on his feet while trying to put his key fob from the gym into his front door lock. I sighed and grabbed the key chain from him and began trying the keys, one at a time. This wasn't how I had planned my night. Right on cue, a clap of thunder sounded and I felt a few raindrops start to fall. When I turned to the side, he was right there. Staring at me with those big, brown, sad and soulful eyes and I forgot all about trying to open the door. He was leaning up against the wall of his house, looking so hurt and so lost.

"Why," he barely whispered.

"Why what, Hardy? Why did I come here?" The rain started to come down just a little bit heavier.

"No, why can't you trust me?"

"It's hard."

"So's grade six, but we all made it through."

I stalled. I wasn't sure where he needed me to go with this, but one thing I was sure was that I didn't want to stay outside much longer. I hated thunderstorms and more than that, I hated getting wet. "Let's get you inside then we can talk."
"I want to talk now."

"Really, Hardy? You want to do this now? Outside in the rain?"

As if the universe really well and truly did hate me just a little bit, the skies opened and it began to pour. Good thing I had already cried off all my non-waterproof mascara. "Great, Hardy. Just fantastic. Are you happy? Now we're all wet."

"Happy? I'm fucking so far from happy." His voice started to escalate. "I haven't been happy for a real long time now." And, he was yelling. Shit, this whole night was turning to crap and now we were involved in a domestic for all the neighbours to hear.

"Calm down. Let's go inside and dry off and talk about this."

He continued yelling as if he hadn't heard a word I said. "The day I met you, I was happy, and even when you were giving me shit, I was still happy. But when you were ready to leave without a single thought to how I would take that, no, I was definitely not very fucking happy!"

There was no point in trying to go inside now. Thunder sounded and lightening lit up the sky and the rain came washing down over both of us, matching our violent hearts perfectly.

I stepped up right into his personal space and let loose all the anger and fear I had been harbouring inside my soul for so long. "It's your fault."

"What's my fault?"

I waved my hand carelessly around. "This whole crazy mess we're in. You made me fall for you, Hardy. You and your adorable dog. You and your brown eyes, beautiful body and sweet and loving soul. It was all your fault."

He got right back in my personal space, something I would have never let any other soul into. "My fault? Have you lost your mind? Maybe it's time you felt something other than fear, huh? Why don't you try for once to be vulnerable and let that stupid assed, hard shell take off for once. Why don't you man up and try being open to falling in love with someone who will love you back. And treat you with the care and compassion you deserve? Why don't you let the time come to take your fucking life back, and not wreck the man who was only trying to accomplish that Herculean task."

He wiped a hand across his face and it was hard to tell if it was rainwater or tears he was wiping away. I just stood there, I had no words left. He was right. He was so dead right that he had stopped me in the middle of my tirade. He knocked all the wind right out of my sails and I hung my head. He had beat me to what I had driven over here to tell him, but why didn't that surprise me? He had, in the two months we had known each other, figured me out better than anyone I knew. And I had hurt him. It was cruel and it was cold and I did it thinking I was protecting him, but I was only protecting myself.

I now had the same mix of salt water and rain flowing down and around my face and knew I wasn't going anywhere. I reached over and tucked my fingers underneath his defeated chin. He raised his chin but his eyes stayed trained on the ground between us. "I have to protect myself, Red. You can't have your heart ripped out of your chest and not understand the dangers in repeating that act after you work so hard to gently put it back in where it came from."

"Hardy, look at me."

No response. "Hardy," I spoke a little bit more forcefully. "Look at me."

He heaved a sigh large enough to move his shoulders around. "I can't do this, Frankie. I can't do this knowing."

"Hardy, fucking look at me." My voice cracked and the pleading began. "Please, sweetheart. I have some important stuff to tell you. If when I'm done and you still can't stand the site of me, I'll go and move and you won't have to see me around. So please," I tugged on his chin again. "Can you please give me your eyes?"

Slowly he lifted those beautiful brown eyes to meet my crazy assed green eyes and I could finally clearly see the damage I had done. I moved my hand up the side of his face, feeling his stubble that I loved so much but had never told him. I felt the soft skin around his eyes and then I moved one finger downwards to trail along his top lip.

"I hate myself. Ok? I hate everything about me. I once thought I was a strong, smart girl who would one day grow into a strong, smart woman, but I played myself. My parents knew, they knew way before I did, that I would cave. I would give in to their relentless scheming and strategizing to get me with Patrick. They knew that he would win me over and they would join forces to make our family even more powerful."

"I'm sick to my stomach. I can't think about myself without thinking about how I let them play me and steer me towards their end game. I make me sick. Then after all that I promised myself I would never be and do, I go and blindly follow the man I reviled into an abusive relationship. And I made excuses for his behavior, and I laughed it off and I worked my ass off to make him love me even more than I thought he did."

I wiped away the mix of tears and rain and snot and my vision blurred. We were sopping wet and yet there was something in the way I felt that made me warm. I was giving a voice to all the self-loathing and hatred I had felt over the past twenty years and it was like my own private train wreck, that I couldn't stop if I wanted to. Hardy reached for me but I held my hands up to hold him back.

"Please, just let me finish. I need to say this. I need to try to make you understand."

I couldn't tell if he was crying or a victim of the rain like me anymore, but giving in to his offer of help wasn't something I could do. He leaned back against the wall, turning to look out at the yard, away from my eyes. The rain was relentless, pounding down, stinging my arms like tiny needles, over and over again. It didn't matter. He mattered. This, now, it mattered.

"I was everything I always said I wasn't going to be, Hardy. I turned into my mother and I had no idea how to turn back. I'm still her. Still running, still pretending to be what I think everyone needs me to be. I know everyone wants me to be strong and come forward, I know everyone wants me to tell the world what a slime ball Patrick is. I know you want me to forget about him and be with you and I hate myself, because I haven't been able to do any of those things. I'm weak, Hardy. Weak. I run. Run from him, run from you, run from my family and I'm especially good at running from myself."

I shifted to face him and took a deep breath and finished what I had come to say. "So, look, um, I'm an idiot. I'm done hating myself and blaming him. I'm taking back my life." I waved my pointer finger up and around for emphasis and let it land right in the centre of his chest. "And I'm taking you back. Sorry, you don't get to walk away from me today, Hardy Hanson. I've waited too long to find you and this," I waved the finger between us, "this hasn't even really gotten started. I've called my real estate agent and told her to stop the negotiations on the place I had found, I called George and told her that she could find me here and I really have no one else to talk to as Sam is in Ireland. Other than the police. I think I really need to talk to the police."

I had done it. I said what I needed to say and now it was up to him. I stood there, both of us getting completely drenched, and stared at him. He was scaring the shit out of me. He wasn't moving, he wasn't looking at me, he had his eyes closed and was looking to the sky. Dammit, I was so stupid. Why did I say all those thing? No guy alive wanted to hear a girl that was into him was also bat shit crazy and refusing to let him break up with her.

"Hardy?"

Nothing. No response. "Hardy, please. Say something. I'm sorry if I just blindsided you, but I couldn't leave without seeing you one last time."
Finally, he tilted his head back down and opened his eyes, but still, I couldn't get a read on him. He matched me, stare for stare, and then started stalking me. Slowly, one foot in front of the other, until he was toe to toe with me again.

"Hardy, wh-"
"Stop talking. It's my turn now."

I felt heat pool between my legs and wondered where this was going to lead. He began to move forward again, only this time, he moved me with him, forcing me to match his steps, except now I was travelling backwards. His eyes held mine and they were electric. Fully charged and ready to ignite and I was mesmerized. There was suddenly nothing more I wanted than to be burned by Hardy Hanson, standing here, in the rain, in his uniform that was currently plastered to every fine square inch of his body. He moved me backwards until I felt the wall of the house stop me, yet he still moved forward. He leaned into me, boxing me in with his hands on either side of my head and his forehead against mine, keeping me in place.

He spoke, barely above a whisper, but I heard everything he said with clarity. "Here's what's going to happen now. Now, you're coming inside with me, then I'm going to strip you down and then you're going to do the same to me. Then I'm going to pick you up, throw you in my bed and keep you there until tomorrow, when we will come up for air. Then and only then will discuss all the guts you just spilled on my front porch."

"Wh-"
"Shush, babe. I said it was my turn to talk. I'm wet, cold, angry, happy, excited, totally fucking turned on, but most of all, so fucking in love with you, even if you just told me we were over and you never wanted to see me again, I'd just smile and let my delusions take over and take you to bed as if you never said a thing, 'cause I'm done being nice. I'm done letting you think. You're mine and it's about time you finally figured that out."

He closed the gap between us with a mouth that was backing up every damn word he just gave me. His mouth attacked mine with a force I hadn't been expecting from my kind and gentle Hardy. Apparently I needed to find some new adjectives to describe Hardy. Demanding, sexy, hot, oh and talented with tongue. He swept his lips against mine in a kiss filled with so much longing and agony, I knew he meant every word he said. He was in control of this kiss and he wanted me to feel all of what he was feeling. It was the most passionate kiss I had ever experienced and it was blowing my mind.

His tongue invaded my mouth and tore apart my soul. This was where I was meant to be, not running. No more running.

Chapter 31

Frankie

He grabbed my bottom and lip and tugged me off the wall, grabbed my hand and pulled me further towards the door. He grabbed the keys back from me, fumbled around trying to find the right one, and finally inserted into the door successfully.

Not waiting around for formalities, he spun me around so I was facing his hall, lifted my arms and held them straight up with one hand. The other hand grabbed a hold of my sopping wet shirt and tugged it upwards. I was desperate to reach back and wrap my arms around his neck, giving him easier access to my body. Turned out he didn't need my help. He got my shirt up as far as he could, let go of my wrists to grab both sides of the top and tug it all the way off.

Before I could react and become an active participant, he grabbed my hands and guided them back until they were wrapped around his neck as if he could read my mind. He made quick work of my bra, unclasping it at the tiny junction between my breasts, giving him complete control of my upper body.

I sighed and leaned back against his body, giving him my weight, trusting him body, mind and soul to take me where he needed to. He cupped my breasts in each hand, gently kneading the nipples until they came alive for him. He bent his head down and began to nibble on my ear whispering his version of sweet nothings to me. He could have been reciting the dictionary for all I knew, but he made it sound like he was reading the Kama sutra. It had been so long since anyone had touched me like this. I pushed all my psychobabble to the back of my brain and decided to pull it out later to analyze why I was all in with Hardy. I trusted him with every single cell inside of me.

His hands left my breasts and criss-crossed around my waist, molding me to him. It was then I realized two things. He really, like I mean, really wanted me and he was so wet, we were standing in a puddle made from our rain soaked clothes.

I spun around in his arms and pulled him in for a heated kiss. It was clear there was going to be a lot of back and forth fights for control with us. My hands were travelling down towards his amazing ass, when he shifted us back towards the wall. Pushed up against the wall, I had nowhere I could go, he had me trapped, but I never felt threatened. It was as if Hardy had the power to erase all the bad and replace the same actions with only good and loving intentions.

He had stilled while I was lost in myself. I could see the fear in his eyes and I knew it was my turn. Never taking my eyes off his, I slowly lifted my hands to the collar of his shirt and began to unbutton the uniform that represented all this man was to me and everyone else surrounding him. Just for one night, I intended to strip him of his sense of responsibility and his constant need to protect and find the man underneath it all. The man who held his anger in, who was raw and passionate and all the things I wanted so badly to unleash on my tortured soul.

My hands began to fumble in their hurry to undress him. He remained still, not sure what his role was going to be at this point. He seemed happy to let me take control so take it I did.

I finally got the damned buttons undone and ripped the shirt from his body getting my first chance at touching this masterpiece in front of me. He dropped his arms to his side and took in a deep breath as I explored the hard planes of his chest. The sprinkling of hair across his upper body felt electric underneath my fingertips and I followed it down towards his waistband where the trail disappeared into regions yet to be explored.

I leaned forward and placed soft kiss in the centre of his chest, needing just a moment to collect myself before I went full force on this man. I felt him place his hands along my neck, gently asking me to look up at him. God, those eyes. How could I have been so stupid? Why had I run so fast to get away from them? They could see me and they couldn't care less what they saw. They loved me and all my flaws.

Our mouths collided again, renewed from the break and this time, I was unafraid of the power I felt from Hardy. I gave it right back to him as our tongues and bodies entwined around each other. He pulled me off the wall and picked me up so my legs automatically wrapped around him. He carried me as if I weighed next to nothing down the hall, kicking open the door to his bedroom.

He walked up to his bed and I untangled my legs and landed softly on his mattress. He quickly shed his pants and soaking wet socks and boots and fell on top of me, picking up right where we left off. His right hand reached in between us to unbutton my jeans, however, being soaked and plastered to my skin, the sexiness of this striptease hit rock bottom. Those jeans, they were stuck. We struggled for a minute or so, trying to ignore the stuckness of said jeans, but then, I totally lost my mind and burst into a fit of the giggles at the look on Hardy's face. He rolled off of me and I wiggled my way out of the chastity jeans and tried my hardest to get the momentum back.

All I had to do was take one eye opening look at Hardy, lying beside me, naked with the exception of his boxer briefs, that left absofuckinglutely nothing to the imagination.

"Eyes up here, beautiful."

I looked up at him, embarrassed to have been caught staring. He was smiling that gorgeous dimpled grin of his. "Ok, we need a reset. Let's try this again."

He straddled my hips, while simultaneously stretching my arms above me, trapping them there with his wrist. All thought of my sticky jeans left my brain and he was all I could comprehend. His touch, seemingly everywhere, took away my nerves. His free hand trailed lazily down, brushing against my sensitive inner arm, waking up my nipple as it travelled over my sensitive breast, not stopping, but continuing on its journey. His fingers slowed their frantic pace when they encountered my hip, stopping altogether at the junction of my inner thigh and their final destination.

Deep breath, Frances. Lock this shit down. I refused to freak out. He was the first for me for so many things lately, but this was a big one for me. I knew I wasn't turning back, but how easy it would be for me to move forward remained to be seen.

He sensed my apprehension and moved in for a sweet kiss, which when it came, I knew was definitely not what my body needed. I needed Hardy to erase every trace of Patrick. I needed it like I needed my next breath.

I opened my eyes and willed him with every ounce of my being to get him to open his eyes. I knew if I spoke, it would break the spell, so we were going to have to rely on our non-verbal cues.

My mojo was working it seemed, as his eyes slowly opened. I poured all my hopes and dreams into one smoldering look, begging him to understand what I needed, before I totally ruined the mood with my stupid tears again.

It appeared he could add mind reader to his resume, as he practically jumped on my mouth and instantly consumed all my fears and left only a simple confidence in his wake. Before I could convince my brain to head back into the fear zone, he had moved his project into fast forward.

His hand came around my back and reached inside my panties and cupped my ass. It was just what I needed. I wiggled and lifted and helping him shimmy off my underwear, finally leaving me completely naked and open to him. He sensed I needed the movement to keep happening. There would be no stopping and staring this time. I had to keep the momentum up or else my brain would take advantage of the gap in action and send me straight back to insecurity town. Population, me.

He came in for another passionate kiss, tugging and pulling on my bottom lip, plunging in and out with his tongue so hard and so fast, I hardly noticed when he slipped a finger inside me. I broke free from his lips and moaned, sent over the edge in a way I never knew I could be.

He forced me back to meet his mouth, continuing his attack. Tongue and finger in perfect sync, driving me crazy and making me squirm and whimper. I did not whimper, this was another first for me. This man was turning me inside out. I felt him everywhere, I couldn't get enough of him. No man I had been with had ever taken the time to explore me. To feel me, to excite me. I was overwhelmed with sensations firing off and turning me into another creature. One who was wanton, crazed and moaning like a sex pro. What the hell was happening to me?

I had never experienced an orgasm during sex. Yes, I was part of that percentage of women who, as I clearly saw it now, were with men who just had no clue or couldn't have cared less. Patrick fell into that last category.

I could feel it coming, fast, hard and incredibly hot. The warmth heated my belly and threatened to lite me on fire. He suddenly added his thumb, sweeping it right across my clit and the sparks took off and sent me over the edge, crying out like a porn star for goodness sakes. My breath came in short bursts, my eyelids fluttered and my hands grasped his biceps, hanging on for dear life.

Slowly, I began my descent back to normal world and felt my face heat up and a blush spread across my chest and up my neck. I dared to peek at him out of one eye, hoping to find he wasn't preparing to exit quickly thanks to my verbal wantonness.

I was good. He was grinning like the caveman he let loose every once in a while. "Feeling pretty good about yourself now, are you?"

"You sounded like you were into it a wee bit." I shrieked and tried to roll over. "You're misunderstanding my words, babe. I loved those noises you made. And yeah, if that makes me a caveman, that so be it, but I gotta say, hot. Crazy hot."

I squirmed my hands free of his grip and grabbed his face and dug in with my lips. It was time to show him exactly how unafraid I was to go there with him. To show him how much he meant to me, and to show him that I was falling in love with him, so deeply, I may never find my way back. Not that I ever wanted to. I had no idea a man like Hardy had even existed before and I could feel the sadness creeping in that I hadn't discovered a love like this well before my thirty-fifth birthday.

Before that sadness could take hold and wreck our night, I gave a little shove and rolled us over. It was my turn to make an attempt at holding his hands up and away from us. "Keep 'em up where I can see 'em."

Lame. So very lame. But I was trying. Having a partner that actually asked me what I needed, then gave me what I needed and willingly lay still and let me explore was so new to me and I was super nervous. Thirty five and never had an orgasm not given as a prezzie to myself. Super lame.

He still had his boxers on and that was going to have to be rectified. I was terrified, but determined and this must have been written all over my face. He lowered his hands to frame my face and smiled a sad, sweet smile. "Babe, don't overthink this and if you're not ready, we'll wait." He softly brushed his lips across mine, ending in a delicious burn across my bottom lip from the sharp beginnings of his beard. "Love you."

Those whispered words were all the encouragement I needed. I was at the edge and jumping was my only option.

It wasn't pretty. I fell on top of him as I was shifting my arms down to seductively remove his boxers. It turned out to be as sexy as a wet fish flopping around on his mid-section. I was all arms and no co-ordination. Trying not to laugh, he was shaking and it wasn't helping at all. "Sorry," I whispered.

Finally, someone in the universe took pity on me and gave me the brilliant idea to roll us to our side. Front to front, I wasn't balancing myself on top of him and I could get a grip on those shifty boxers. I dug my thumbs in and gave a good yank down. I had to abandon my plan of slowly inching his undies down bit by bit while I gazed lovingly into his eyes. The boxers were soaking wet, I was soaking wet for that matter and I felt like my time was running out. I needed to get Hardy naked, pronto.

Now came the hard part. With my gaze lowered, I raised my terrified and shaking right hand to hover above his chest. Except I couldn't make it connect. What the hell was wrong with me?

I felt a gentle hand tuck beneath my chin and push upwards so my eyes eventually had nowhere to go but up. They slammed into his and it was all I needed to release my quivering hand and move it forward to brush up against his chest. My fingers stroked and explored the short dusting of hair across his body, while still holding our connection with our eyes.

My hands increased their pace, becoming frantic, searching for something they weren't aware they needed. I broke our staring contest by falling into his mouth with my body. Pushed up against Hardy, I could feel his love and patience radiating from him and I was more determined than ever to push my fears aside and ignite. Burn up. From the inside out.

Our lips came together and fused and pulled and tried to fuse again. Our hands were erratically tracing the lines of our bodies and our hips were colliding again and again, frantically trying to fit together. This was passion, this was energy, this was love.

Hardy scooped an arm under me and shifted us up and turned us so we were lying in the bed properly and he could easily reach over me and into his side drawer. He grabbed a condom and rolled it on and I tried my hardest not to stare, but I was completely unsuccessful. It had been awhile and well, you know, that thing looked kinda big.

I laid back, closed my eyes and let my other senses take over. And it was bliss. I could feel his heat as he hovered over me. I reached up and around him to give the signal that all systems were a go. I could do this and I was going to do it with Hardy.

He rocked a little, back and forth, rubbing and creating friction up against my clit. I had never experienced an orgasm during sex, so two in one night was an entry in the diary I didn't have, but needed to get first thing. He picked up the pace and I began to feel the warm electricity coursing through me. His kiss took me by surprise, I was so focused on not wigging out. He mirrored the in and out movements of his lower half and before I knew it, he had reached down between us and got himself in the ready position.

I realized he was holding himself up off of me and if I had opened my eyes, I would probably see him looking and waiting for permission to move forward. With Herculean strength, I opened my eyes, and it was all he needed to see, as he surged forward. I gasped at the invasion while at the same time, moved my hips up to meet him.

"Baby," he whispered.

"Mhm?"

"You O.K.?"

"Are you going to keep moving?"

"Yeah."

"Then I'm good."

He surged back in and we didn't look back. My hands were everywhere. Touching, grabbing, pinching and kneading his fantastic body. I wasn't much into comparing, but damn, he beat any other guy I had ever been with in all areas of competition. His back was smooth and rippled beneath my touch and his ass was perfection. That's it. That's all I could come up with.

Our pace increased as did the pressure mounting in my belly. The warmth was spreading and I squirmed to get closer to Hardy, but my end goal seemed totally out of reach.

I guess I should never play poker. My thoughts and emotions are most often written all over my face and it looked like right now was no exception. Hardy moved his hand between us to place just enough pressure to send me to the edge and give me the huge push I needed. I flew. I never knew it could be like this.

His hand quickly moved to brace himself against his momentum and he joined me over that edge. I needed to be careful. I am pretty sure tears after sex were never appropriate, especially for a second time. Even happy, can't believe I gave myself this second chance kind of tears. Nope. Not gonna happen Frances. Hold it together and lock those in nice and tight.

Hardy nudged me with his nose, up against my nose breaking me from my focus and a damn tear made a run for it right over my eye and down my face. Just one tear, so maybe I could nonchalantly reach around and wipe it away without him noticing.

"I love you, Frances Dorothy Cain."

"Jesus, Hardy. You just took all the sex appeal I was trying to hold onto away with that. How do you know my full name?"

"Driver's license. Are you crying sweetheart?"

I used that moment to reach up and wipe away that damn loner tear. He didn't say a word. Just wrapped me up in his safe arms, giving me one more stupid reason to wonder why I had been holding onto my need to run from someone as amazing as this.

Chapter 32

Frankie

You know the feeling you get when you just know someone is staring at you? Yeah, that feeling. I must have finally drifted off but it couldn't have been for very long, because it was still pitch black outside when I cracked an eye open. Hardy was staring at me with a look on his face that reminded me of peace, irreverence and incredulity.

"Hey," I whispered. "You ok? Can't sleep?"

"I'm good. Just have better things to do than sleep."

"Oh, like be a creepy stalker?"

"Something like that."

I reached up and traced his jaw delicately. I was afraid something was wrong, but more afraid to ask.

"Do you have this happen often?"

"What, a beautiful woman in my bed who I can't stop looking at? Ya, all the time."

"Hilarious. I meant, do you have trouble sleeping at night?"
He nodded yes.

"Me too. I've become a pretty light sleeper in the past few years. We both know why I can't sleep, but why you?"

"I've just suffered from nightmares ever since the fire. I've gotten pretty good at operating without sleep. But tonight's a little different. I can't sleep because there is an amazingly beautiful woman in my bed who I have loved since the moment I met her. The fantasy of this moment has gotten me through quite a few long and lonely nights the past month. You have no idea what having you here is doing to me."

I could feel what it was doing to him on the side of my leg, but decided to let that go and focus on, "the moment we met? Really Hardy? You believe in love at first site?"

He looked uncomfortable and he probably wished he had never begun this conversation. "I've got a reputation to uphold and I will deny it if ever asked by anyone who is not you, but yes, I do. It's the only way I fall."
"Are you for real?"

He just smiled and leaned in to plant a sweet kiss on my nose. I was so glad I pulled my head out of my ass and chased him down. Hardy was the kind of guy you met and never let go of. I was stupid to think I could remove him from my system. I didn't know how long it was going to last, but I was done thinking I didn't deserve his love. I deserved it. I wasn't sure I could give him the kind of love he deserved back, but I was going to have to figure that out later.

I yawned and he yawned back and I flipped over and snuggled in, letting him spoon me again. I grabbed his hand and gave it a quick kiss. "Try to sleep Hardy. I only have room for one stalker in my life right now. I can't sleep with you staring at me like that."

I felt his breath hot up against my neck and ears. "Night baby. Sleep tight."

We settled in for our first night together and if I could see myself, I am sure I would see a grinning lunatic but I had honestly never been happier than this moment right now.

Chapter 30

Hardy

What the fuck just happened? I woke up pissed off at the world. Our break up had me tied up in knots and I was so angry that I had been on a bender when I wasn't at work all week. Add to that, my mom and sister had been bugging me about Frankie and showed up at my door this morning. They were worried I hadn't been answering the phone or texts and came to see if I was still alive.

I had wished I wasn't for a few hours and then was pissed at myself for thinking that. Then the fuckers staged some sort of intervention after work and I freaked out. Drove to the Beach Club and drowned my sorrows. When my phone got a text while I was there, I almost ignored it, but something made me glance down.

I instantly got worried, even though I was blitzed. It was from my neighbour across the street. I've never been so thankful to live across from a nosy old woman since I had moved in. She told me that a car had pulled into my drive and no one had gotten out for quite a while and she was concerned.

I texted her back and asked for the make of the car and when she perfectly described Frankie's car, against all my better judgement, I called a cab. And now, I was here, with my Frankie, spooning in my bed. I felt like beating my hands on my chest and screaming like the caveman she often accused me of being.

She felt amazing up against me and if wasn't recovering from a weeklong after work bender, I would make sure round two began right now. I was also thankful Chuck wasn't here. She was currently occupying his favourite spot. He snuck up into my bed when the rain and thunder came.

I tightened my grip and leaned into her hair and sent up a silent prayer to Sarah and the universe for her. Now all I had to do was figure out a way to keep her safe and stop her from running. It was time to find that asshole and rid her of him for good.

Chapter 33

Frankie

The sun streaming in through the windows woke me the next day, that and the snoring symphony next to me. Hardy must have been in a really deep sleep. Knowing he needed his sleep, I quietly crept from the bed and pulled on a t-shirt of Hardy's.

First up would be making coffee, then breakfast. I set about getting things ready and while doing so, turned on my phone to see what I had missed while having a Hardy Hanson sleepover.

My phone beeped that a text had come in. That was really strange. Only a handful of people had my cell number. I swiped it open and dropped it immediately. "Fuck." How in the hell had he found me? I had been so careful, but clearly not careful enough.

I clicked the text open again and looked at the series of pictures. The first was a picture of me leaving my house getting into my car yesterday. The second was of me parked in Hardy's driveway and the third was of Hardy and I in the rain last night. The caption below the pictures read, I see you Little Rabbit.

Think, Frances. Think. I didn't want Hardy to know. He would go and get himself hurt or worse. I had to figure out how to take care of this myself. I decided to text him back.

    I didn't know stalker was now on your political platform.

Lame, I knew, but I had to show him I wasn't afraid of him anymore. The phone immediately buzzed back with an incoming text. I started biting my nails. Shit, I was out of my element here. I wasn't sure if I should ignore it, call the cops or wake up Hardy.

I chose to be an idiot and swiped open the phone again.

    Bitch, you think you can beat me? You think your pretty new boyfriend can protect you? His t-shirt looks like shit on you sweetheart.

I dropped the phone and took off. I ran to the back deck that opened onto the beach and checked the lock and wished Hardy wasn't a guy. A woman would have curtains for privacy back here. His house was wide open to the beach. Next I ran to the front door to check the lock and proceeded to check each window and close all the shutters.

I slowed my pace, as I went back to Hardy's bedroom. I didn't want to alarm him, so I needed to get my shit together. I paused at the threshold to his room and took a moment to take him in. He was spread flat out on his back, his curls flying all over. Arms cocked up at his sides and his mouth was wide open and making the most horrendous noises. He was adorable and amazing and mine to protect. Patrick wouldn't hurt him, I would make sure of it.

I crawled onto the bed and slipped under the covers and snuggled into his side, wrapping my arm across his hard, rippled body. I poked him in the side a bit to wake him and stop the awful snoring. He sputtered, turned into me and smiled in his sleep.

"Morning sunshine. Was I snoring?"

"Like a trucker."

"Damn. Sorry babe."

"It's super attractive. Don't worry. I'm surprised it hasn't caught on with the ladies yet."

He smiled a sleepy, sexy smile and slipped an arm around me and his leg in between mine. "I'm keeping you in my bed Frankie, so you better learn to find my snoring a peaceful reminder of the babe sleeping beside you. You'll learn to love it. Snoring is hot."

I laughed and pinched him and we attacked each other, tickling, trying to get the other to surrender. Eventually, our playful wrestling turned into something else and before I knew it, he had flipped me under him and his tongue was trying to tickle my tonsils.

I wrapped my arms around his waist and down to his ass and pushed him against my open legs. And froze. Hardy's curtains were open. Shit. I needed to somehow get them closed without raising suspicion and keeping our sexmentum moving in the right direction.

I rolled us over and scooted towards the edge of the bed. This wasn't going to work. I was going to have to come up with plan B.

"Hey, could we close the blinds?"

He stopped and looked at me questioningly. "Sure, why?"

"Well, it's daylight?"

He grinned. "Yeah, and?"

"And well, um, the whole beach can see in?"

He hopped off and grabbed a hold of the curtains and gave a little tug to each one and we were once again wrapped up in the darkness. I loved that he had room darkening liners to help him sleep at all times of the day. At least one set of windows in this house had some privacy.

"Now, where were we?" I scooted over to let him back and in made my very best effort to push my evil ex out of my mind. He couldn't hurt us in here. He wouldn't dare.

I felt a tug on my nipple, and I realized I had zoned out on him and gave myself a mental shake. This gorgeous man was working on giving me an orgasm and the least I could do was be present.

He moved to give my other nipple some attention, being the equal opportunity lover that he is and I nearly came right then and there. I was so inexperienced that its' almost embarrassing.

I raked my hands through his hair and scratch the surface of his scalp with my nails. He moved to trail kisses down between my breasts towards my stomach and it's obvious he got the memo. Head south immediately.

His hot breath left trail of fire as it moved towards its destination. Oh God. He's headed there. The place where no man has gone before him. I was so embarrassed. Why in the world-.

His tongue hits me right in my centre. Oh, I see now. That's why. "Hardy," I whispered. I could feel him smiling down there and a slow burn of redness crept up my neck.

"Are you laughing at me?"

He didn't respond. He was busy. I got that message loud and clear when he gave my clit a particularly strategic tug which helped me forget all about being embarrassed and shot me right down a path that was surely heading straight to heaven.

My hands left his hair and gripped the sheets on either side of me when I came with a force so strong, it had me gasping for my next breath.

Slowly, I released my death grip on the sheets and wound my hands around his chest to pull him up towards me. He had a boyish grin on his face like he was oh so proud of himself, and I suppose, rightly so. He was the first man to give that to me. He had gone where no man had gone before and the results were spectacular.

He flopped back down beside me and propped his head in his hand and began tracing his finger lightly across my body. "Hardy, you need to stop touching me. We will never get out of bed if you keep doing stuff like that."

He just grinned again, got that little boy twinkle all kicked into high gear, and scooped an arm under me and swung me up on top of him.

"Ah, I see. This is your plan. Get me nice and relaxed and then drop me down on top of you with the hopes your aim in on target."

He burst out laughing and moved in for an obvious tickle attack but I was so ready for him. In every way. I grabbed at his hands and pinned them down beside his stretched out body. I wiggled back until I was positioned just right. He suddenly tore his hands away from mine and grabbed onto my hips, stilling them in mid-air.

"Frankie, sweetheart. Are you on the pill?"

"Yes, to regu-"

He picked my hips up and slammed them down onto him, more than ready to move forward. I guess he didn't care that I had irregular periods.

This too was going to be a new experience for me. I hadn't been on top either. Hardy was a whole bundle of new experiences for me, good and bad, but whatever happened, I knew he would always put my needs and wants first. Oh yeah, that was new to me too.

I picked up the pace, anxious to explore the new us. My body began to take over, instinctively knowing what it needed to do.

"Eyes, Red. Look at me."

I briefly glanced down at him, but quickly looked away. I was terrified of the eye lock. Way too personal. Staring into his eyes while making love seemed so overwhelming that I felt a panic attack welling up inside of me and lost my concentration.

"Relax, Frankie. Babe, look at me. Nothing bad is going to happen to you. Just, please, look at me."

Nothing bad was going to happen my ass. I had been surrounded by darkness since conception. I needed to protect Hardy from it, but he seemed determined to drag me kicking and screaming into his light.

He slowly reached a hand up to tuck my crazy hair softly behind my ear, leaving his hand there, cupping my cheek. "Baby, look at me. Come on, you can do this. I know you can. I'm here and I'm not going anywhere."

I tried to resume our activity, but he stilled my hips with his other hand on my hip. "Hardy," I whispered. "I can't-"

"No, you can." He lifted his hand from my hip to cup my chin and tug it towards him, forcing my eyes to follow.

"How do I do this, Hardy?"

"With me. Together."

"He's coming for me."

"Don't care. I've got you, babe. I've got this."

"But-"

He slipped a finger over my lips, stilling the urge to protest against the onslaught of feelings. He smiled, a shy, tiny smile. "My Red. Hair wild and on fire, heart locked down and fireproof. When we're together in our bed, we're not thinking of anything else but each other, ok? It's you," he lightly kissed the corner of my mouth, "and me." He moved over to the other corner and placed a tiny kiss there. "I've got you babe." He was whispering and pulling me closer to his chest, placing tiny, soft kisses along my jaw up towards my ear. "Let go. Let me catch you."

At this point, I really had no idea what he was saying and I felt like he could tell me monkeys were dancing in the corner of the room, it wouldn't matter. I was so turned on and couldn't remember why I was holding back five minutes ago. He nipped at my earlobe, tugging me even closer. The sting reminded me we were still joined and my anxiety had interrupted us.

Ever so slowly, I gave him what he was asking for. I gave him my body, bared my soul and let him protect me. Screw the feminist shit, screw the isolation. I needed him. I needed him to love me, to take care of me, to show me men were kind, sexy creatures. I needed him to give me all that and more.

Chapter 34

Frankie

I felt those eyes on me again. I was so exhausted, I was quite possibly made of lead. I couldn't lift an arm, but I could manage to turn my head towards the magnetic pull of his stare. "Hey, stalker boy, you're staring again."

He had a sheen to him that made his smooth skin glow. I was having trouble focusing, yet again. He was propped up, facing me with a sheet barely covering anything that mattered. "One, two, three. Eyes on me."

I laughed. "Were you a teacher in a past life?"

"My sister. She's got oodles of kids. I can't wait for you to meet them."

Nope, not gonna get scared. Meeting kids didn't mean a lifetime commitment, Frankie. Get a hold of yourself. "I would love to meet them one day."

He smiled. "Nice job with the not freaking out. Now, let's get our lazy asses out of bed and eat something. I have to go into work today. What are you going to do?"

"Not sure. I'm going to head home and paint."

"Nudes?"

I rolled my eyes. "I don't do nudes, buddy."

He rolled on top of me. "What can I do to commission a nude of my girl. What's it gonna cost me?"

"You can't afford me."

He raised an eyebrow. "Oh, excuse me miss fancy pants artist." He continued rolling, heading off the bed, poking me in the side on his way by. I giggled and then forgot to speak as I got my first good look at his rear assets. He was staring between the gap in his curtains, giving me an unobstructed, bright lights view of his perfectly contoured ass. Sigh.

What wasn't so amazing was that he was looking out the window. I didn't need to give Patrick any more ammo when it came to me and my new life without him. He had been chasing me for the better part of a year now and looking at this naked, strong man in front of me, it was time to let him know he had come to the end of the road. I just had to figure out how to do that in a way that would keep both Hardy and I whole.

He turned and I once again forgot how to speak. If I thought his rear view was spectacular, the front was eclipsing my eyes. I might go blind if I stared at it too long. What an idiot I had become around him. I needed to get back some of my reserved contemplation and lock down the restless hormones.

He just stood there, as if he knew the internal monologue I was listening to was waxing poetic to his bits and pieces on display. "Can I help you?" He asked, raising his quirky, cool left eyebrow.

"I'm good."

He smirked and turned and walked away. "I'm going to put coffee on. I've got to go in about thirty minutes. Need a ride home?"

He was unfortunately getting dressed. I guess our little love nest was going to have to let the real world in. "No, I'm going to drive myself. I already put the coffee on by the way. I've got some stuff I have to do and need my car to do it."

"Ok. Are you going to come back tonight?"

My cheeks got hot and he grinned wickedly in response. "There she is. My baby wants to come back tonight." He bent over and gave me a quick, hard kiss and turned and headed out to make coffee.

I blew my hair off my face and flopped back down into his bed and wondered how I was going to keep myself from diving into this fire with Hardy headfirst.

We quickly got ready to head out to our respective jobs, acting as if we were used to being together as a couple. We downed a cup or two of coffee, he got dressed in his uniform and I made do with a t-shirt of his and my crunchy jeans that had dried stiff from last night.

"Why are all the curtains closed?"

Shit. "Ah well, when I got up this morning and you were peacefully, snoring away in your bed, the sun was super bright and my brain just wanted dark and cozy."

"Ah. Ok. Mind if I open up a few of them again? I love the view here when I'm drinking coffee."

"Actually, I have kind of a headache. Could we just keep them closed?" Great, Frankie. Starting out day one of this relationship with a big, fat lie. I suck. No, Patrick sucks. He was the reason I had to keep Hardy literally in the dark.

He walked over to me, looking at me kind of oddly. "Sure. We can keep them closed. You feeling ok?"

Great, now he's worried about me and what I was trying to avoid, came to be anyway. "I'm good. Just tired. Ready to go?"

"Yup." He pulled me in for a hug, wrapping his long arms around me and giving me a reassuring squeeze. I could do this. Leaving the house had to happen at some point.

We headed for the door, hand in hand. "Ok, so I'll text you later when I know what time I'm done my shift. Depends on what's going on tonight. Might not be until late. Want me to come to you? Oh, or better still," He bent over and retrieved his spare key and held it out for me. "Here's a key. Why don't you come over sometime and I can act out fantasy number two. Me coming home to you in my bed."

"Sure, I can do that. Do you want me to bring you some dinner?"

He lightly planted a kiss in the center of my mouth. "That sounds amazing. Text me later with my options."

Chapter 35

Frankie

I walked in my door and instantly knew someone had been in there. I had some serious OCD issues and could tell right away that my entry mat was crooked, and the door leading to my spare room was never open like it was right now.

So, I had a decision to make. Back out the door and head to the police, or dive in and get this over with. I decided that today I had begun my quest of living on the edge, why stop now?

I eased my way inside and noticed more things out of place by fractions. I pulled out my phone and started snapping pics, hoping like hell, my shaking hand didn't make everything blurry.

I finally made it into the kitchen and noticed I had a welcome note left on the island. I didn't want to touch it, so I moved to the cabinet and got out a plastic baggy and slipped my hand inside in order to grab the note without disturbing anything on it.

Frances, I am giving you one last chance to come home. You have left me no choice in this matter. Stop playing house and get back to the life you were designed for. I have your envelope. There is no sense going to the police. Stupid girl. When will you learn? You have my number, call me.

I dropped the note and ran to my room and into the closet. Tearing the shoes and clothes out of the way, I finally came to the fireproof box where I kept everything that would free me from this nightmare one day.

"Damn." It came out as a whisper. The box was empty and my security was gone.

"Fuuuucccck," I screamed with rage coming out from the pit of my soul. I threw the box at the wall, leaving a huge dent in it. I screamed at the top of my lungs, needing desperately to stave off the despair creeping in along the edges of my subconscious.

Inside the box I had saved all my proof. Proof that Patrick Marks was a fraud. That the next front runner candidate for the Republican Party leadership was a user. A user of drugs, a user of women and a user of young men. My ex-fiancé liked to show his fans his powerful, charming side, but behind closed doors, he hit his soon to be wife so hard one night, he killed their unborn child. Behind closed doors the youngest Presidential Republican Candidate to seek leadership liked to tie up young men and have his way with them. Right after he did three lines of coke.

And I had the proof. I had been slowly gathering it my whole life. This wasn't something that took me by surprise. No, I knew what I was getting into when I finally gave into the pressure to agree to marry him. No, in fact, I was an enabler. Until the night he took my child. I had photos, videos and finally, physical proof that would ruin him. Doctor's records, police records and humiliating photos of me in ICU after the last time he beat me.

And now, all of it gone. All those years of bearing his torture, just gone, because I was stupid enough to think I could beat him.

I wiped the tears falling down my face and sucked in a huge breath. I heard my phone beep and pulled it out of my pocket.

It was a text from Hardy. How did he always seem to know when I needed him?

>   Miss you.

It was a plain and simple text but said a ton of things to me. I had a someone now. I knew I had always had Sam and George, but I had found a man who loved me, who missed me and who wanted to protect me from the horrors I had coming for me.

I sunk my head in my hands and took in a deep, cleansing breath. That asshole was not going to win. I had changed. I wasn't his door mat any more. Hardy gave me strength and I was going to figure out a way to fight back even though I didn't have the proof I had so painstakingly gathered over the years.

I got up and splashed some cold water on my face, then ran to the kitchen, suddenly filled with a sense of urgency to complete this part of my life and move on. I stuck my hand in the plastic bag, picked up the note, turned the bag inside out and sealed it. I swiped my keys off the counter and took off in my car. I was going to fight fire with fire.

Chapter 36

Frankie

I had just put my phone down and was debating how much to tell Hardy about everything going on with Patrick, when it beeped, alerting me I had another incoming text. I picked it up to retrieve the text and nearly dropped the phone in fear. It was from him.

    I know you're reading this, whore.

I ran around, dropping the blinds, locking the doors and windows, grabbed my purse and ran out the front and into my car. My heart was racing and it made me fumble with my keys, just like I was in a real, live horror movie.

"Damn, damn, damn." I slammed the palm of my hand onto the steering wheel. "Ok, Frances. Calm down. He's not here. He's just messing with you."

I finally got the keys in the ignition and tore out of the driveway, letting my instincts take me directly to the fire station where Hardy worked. It was fifteen minutes away and in my hurry, I hadn't turned off my phone, so I could hear it alerting me to multiple incoming texts as I drove. I worked on focusing my calming energy just like my therapist had taught me. Less stress, more blessed. Less stress, more blessed. God, I cannot believe I was repeating that ridiculous mantra.

My hands were shaking and I was having trouble keeping the car on the road, so I gave in and started repeating those words over and over again. It didn't work for shit. I squealed into the parking lot of the fire station, slammed the car into park and grabbed my phone. Hardy had been talking to his staff while in the bay where the trucks were kept and so had seen me tear in. He met me as I burst out of the car.

"Babe, what's the matter?"

I was so fucking terrified, I couldn't speak. I held out my shaking hand for him to take my phone. He took the phone and tucked it in his pocket and wrapped me in his arms. "Babe," he whispered in my ear, "not gonna ask again, what the fuck is going on? You are scaring the ever loving shit right out of me."

"Read the phone." I hardly recognized my voice. It was barely a whisper. He looked at me like he wanted to yell some more, but thankfully, thought better of it. He swiped my phone open and I could tell he was holding onto some serious rage. His nostrils flared, he chewed his bottom lip and he turned around and dragged me behind him into the station.

We walked past lots of curious eyes, but by the look of things, his guys knew when to give their chief a wide berth. We strode past the truck and went around back into what must have been his office. He sat me in a chair, closed the door and dragged a spare chair up in front of me.

"For starters, you're moving in with me."

"Ok."

He looked like he wanted to say more, but held his tongue. "Now, have you called the police?"

"No."

"Why the hell not?"

"I was scared, Hardy." I would not cry. That bastard can't make this happen to me again. "I didn't think. After I came home and got his note and realized he had been there, my mind went right into preservation mode for me and that doesn't usually involve the police. Then when I got these texts, I took off for here. Please don't be mad at me."

He kicked back the chair he was sitting on and dove for me. "Fuck, Red. Mad at you? What do you take me for?" He worked his free hand through his hair and then back down his face, took a few deep breaths and then started to speak. "Ok, so, you didn't read the other texts past the first one?"

"No."

"'Cause babe, they get a hell of a lot worse and it looks to me like he's found you. Wait, did you say there was a note in your house when you got home? Shit, Frankie, and you didn't think to call the police right then and there?"

I had nothing to say. All my careful plans and hiding all gone to shit in a matter of minutes. The tears I had been holding onto fell freely as Hardy scooped me up and settled me into his lap. He stroked my hair as I cried for all the things I continued to lose thanks to that evil man.

"All I seem to do is cry all over you." I sniffled as I lifted my head.

He just smiled and smoothed back my hair from my face. "Sweetheart, I think you need to let me call the police. There is some pretty disturbing stuff in those texts and he has been trespassing to boot."

I reached for the phone, but he scooted it out of the way. "Can I see?"

"I don't think that's going to help you right this minute."

"But-"

"Trust me, babe. Please, just trust me. That guy is one messed up man." He got up, righted his chair and set it back down in front of me again. He held both my hands in his and gave me a strengthening squeeze. "So, what do you say? First, we call the cops, then, you tell me his full name. No more secrets. No more protecting that scum and no more protecting me. I can take care of myself and I will be taking care of you from this point forward."

It was time. I had come to a crossroads. It looked like I needed more than just Sam and George's help. Patrick had crossed some sort of crazy line and he appeared to not be inclined to stop until he had me eliminated or something.

"Ok, Hardy. Make the call."

He grabbed his desk phone and spun it around to face us and dialled a number other than just plain old 911. Leave it to him to have a direct line to the powers that be.

"Hey, it's Hardy. Yeah, been good. Listen, I've got something I need you to take a look at. Can you get over here real quick?" He paused while whoever was on the other line replied to his demands. "Thanks, Joe. I'll owe you another looks like. Fill you in when you get here." And then he just hung up. If I wasn't so freaked out, I would make some comment on how men and women ask for favours so differently.

He pulled me in again, tucked his arms under my legs and swung me up into his lap. I rested against him and wondered not for the first time, how I had gotten so lucky at finding him. "Do you believe in fate Hardy?"

"Nope."

"Why not?"

"I used to believe in a lot of that kind of stuff, but life had other plans for my beliefs and showed me good shit can go bad really, really fast. What I believe in now is taking chances to live a life I want to live. I have the three most amazing women to show me that."

"Who?"

"My mom, Sarah and you." He placed a chaste kiss on my nose. "My mom always told me to take life by the balls, Hardy."

"Oh my God."

"Yup, that's my mom. Can't wait for you to meet her. And no, do not even do that shit with me right now. You're meeting her. Done."
I sighed.

"Next was Sarah. She wasn't much for that motto while she was alive, but for a long time, I raged at whoever I could blame for her death, until one day, there was this beautiful woman, lying on top of my dog, all crazy red hair flying and sputtering indecent words for everyone to hear." He smiled, dimples out, eyes shining. "She lead Chuck to you and in that moment I thanked her for all I hadn't thanked her for, but most of all, I thanked her for showing me it was time. Shit, I don't believe in fate, but I knew right then and there, you were going to be mine." He buried his face in my neck. "God, I sound like such a lame assed dickhead. What have you done to me?" He laughed out loud and in spite of the circumstances, I laughed right along with him.

"And last but certainly not least, there's you." His eyes took on a warmth that helped me forget where we were and why we were having this conversation. "You got out, when it was nearly impossible for you to believe you could. You've survived horrors and life on your own and you didn't let fear dictate your life. I love that about you and learn more every day how amazing and strong you really are, so, thanks." He smiled and I could have jumped him right there and then, except for the discreet throat clearing that came from the doorway.

Hardy swung us around to face the police officer standing in the door. "That was fast. Joe, come on in." He set me down into my chair and got up to shake hands with Joe and close the door behind him.

"Joe, this is my girlfriend, Frankie. Frankie, meet Joe."

Girlfriend. There it was. I didn't have time to process why a surge of pride and happiness shot through me. I should be running the other way at that term.

Joe reached out a hand and we did the obligatory hand shake and got down to business. I was happy to let Hardy take control this time. Patrick's texts had upset me more than I wanted to admit. I wasn't altogether ready to deal with the implications and fall out from revealing them to the cops.

Hardy started to fill him in. "So, Frankie used to be in a relationship back in LA that became abusive, or maybe always was abusive...."

I began to tune him out and fall into a zone. I only half listened as he told my sad and embarrassing story to this complete stranger. This wasn't a good idea. Patrick usually had the cops eating out of his hands. Who would ever believe me over the powerful, politically perfect, Mr. Patrick Marks.

I was studying my nails and deciding when exactly I would be breaking Hardy's heart by getting the heck out of town, when I finally noticed a lull in their conversation.

"Red? You ok?"

"Sorry, I wasn't really paying attention Hardy." I went back to studying my nails and plotting my escape.

"Babe, Joe needs to ask you a few questions, ok?"

I looked up at him and begged him with my eyes to let this go. Let me go. Nothing good was going to come of this and this Joe guy was going to make me take this public and then we all would regret things. The silence hung over us like an Irish fog, just waiting for the signal to descend and obscure my vision, in the blink of an eye.

"Frankie, sweetheart." Hardy got up and came around his desk, turned me to face him and knelt down to bring us eye to eye. "Hey, it's ok. You don't have to be afraid anymore. We're going to figure this out and bring this asshole down."

"You can't win this Hardy. With Patrick, everybody loses but him."

"Listen, let Joe ask you some questions, then if when he's done, you still aren't comfortable pursuing a case against him, we'll have to respect your wishes. Though, I gotta say, I really need to nail this asshole."

Yet another, dumb tear rolled down my face because I knew. I knew I was screwed. I couldn't let Hardy down. He thought I was some sort of super woman. You could tell he was raised in a house full of woman. He sure had a handle on how to treat a woman and what to say to her to make her fall madly in love with him. Crap on a cracker. I was in love. For realz.

I took a deep, cleansing breath and turned to face Joe. "Let's get started officer. What's your first question?"

Chapter 37

Frankie

We spent a good two hours rehashing as much as I could remember while still skirting around some of the truths I wasn't ready to admit just yet. I gave up Patrick's name and his status and basically made Hardy the happiest man on earth. I gave into his wishes. For him and him alone, I would let go and pursue this investigation as far as we could take it. Which wasn't probably far, but seeing the look on Hardy's face was worth it.

Joe stood up to go and bagged up my phone and the note. It was going into evidence for a bit. Didn't matter. I never wanted to have that number again. Anyone worth my time, would either find me or I knew their number off by heart, and I would find them. We shook hands again and arranged to keep in touch.

Hardy shut the door behind Joe and turned, and leaned against it, giving me the "you're in trouble look".

I went on the defensive right away. "What?"

"What?"

"Hey, I whated you first. Why are you looking at me that way?"

"What way?"

"Like I'm in trouble."

He sauntered over to where I was sitting and crouched down in front of me, steepling his hands and looking very thoughtful. "Why was this the first time I heard the majority of all that shit?"

"Well, it's not exactly running conversation. Come on, give me a break here."

"This stops here, ok?"

He leaned forward and placed his hands on both of my knees. I delicately traced the callouses he had on his knuckles, while trying to figure out what I wanted to say.

"I don't know how to do this, Hardy. I haven't had a healthy, normal relationship before. I've always held things close to my chest. Letting someone else have my issues doesn't come easy to me." I took in a breath and smelled his unique, alluring scent. "So, yeah, I'm sorry I didn't tell you most of the stuff that's been happening lately, if any, but you know now. Are you going to leave? 'Cause I wouldn't blame you." I looked away to the wall. I didn't want to see the judgement in his eyes. I just wasn't sure I could take it.

"Frankie, hey, look at me. Please?"

I reluctantly swivelled my eyes to meet his. "Yes?"

"I'm not going anywhere. You have to know that. You, my girl, are stuck with me. I couldn't stop being with you if I tried my hardest. You're inside of me, babe."

"Ok."

"Ok? That's it?"

"Ok, I'll share this stuff with you. The truth is, when I decided to stay, I knew I would need someone here to lean on. You're him, Hardy. I'm making the decision to let go for a little bit and see what happens. From here on out, I will probably share with you more than you want to know in a day."

"Oh, yeah? Tell me something I don't already know about Frances Cain."

I smiled at my hated name. "Well, for starters, no one calls me Frances, except my mom, and can expect to live afterwards."

He rocked back on his heels. "Is that so?"

"Yup, true story. Oh, and here's something else." I took a hold of his hands and dove in. "I'm scared, Hardy. I don't know what he's going to do next. He's been in my house, he's followed me, and he's become a peeping Tom. I'm full of anxiety and won't be able to sleep and you aren't going to like hanging with me in that condition."

"I thought we already took care of that. You're sleeping at my house, permanently. And you won't be there alone until we catch him and send him back to the pits of hell where he belongs." He got up and pulled me with him. "So, now that that's settled, I need to take you somewhere, but I just need a few minutes to take care of a couple of things. Ok?"

"Where are we going?"

He smiled his oh so cute dimpled smile. "It's a surprise." And waltzed out of his office, out of sight.

Chapter 38

Frankie

We pulled up in front of a sweet ranch style house, in a quiet, residential neighbourhood. Hardy hopped out and ran around to my side to open my door. He still hasn't told me who lives here and why we're here. I'm starting to suspect it's because I won't like his answer.

He grabs my hand and pulls me along towards the front door, when I decided to dig in my heels. "Ok, are you going to tell me why we're here, or am I going to scream like a toddler and throw a tantrum?"

"Scream all you want. We're here now and I drove so you can't run away. This is my mom's house."

At that exact horrifying moment, the front door swung open and a tiny person catapulted out of it, straight into Hardy's body, where he attached himself to his legs. Oh boy. I am so not good with kids. If he's dumping me here and there are children, he's going to decide to dump me somewhere else by the end of the day. Far away. I suck at children.

"Uncle Hardy, are you gonna play ball with me?"

"Can't today, buddy." He picks him up and easily balances the boy in his arms, while never letting go of my hand. "I've gotta get back to work."

"Then why are you here, and who is she?"

"She is Frankie and I'm here to drop her off for a visit."

"Frankie's a boy's name."

"Not this time around, Luke." He gave my hand a tug and propelled us forward as best he could while holding Luke and pulling me. "This Frankie is a beautiful, redheaded girl."

"Girls are gross," Luke claimed.

"Well, not really buddy. Especially not this one."

A woman appeared at the door and I started to panic. This wasn't me. I didn't do good girlfriend. I had to make Hardy take me back.

"Hardy, sweetheart. What are you doing here?" His mom, at least, I was assuming this was his mom, was shorter than Hardy and looked to be around sixty years old. She had stylish dark hair, cut into a chic bob. She ushered us through the front door and into a living room. Midway into the room, she stopped and seemed to realize I was there.

"I'm sorry, where are my manners? You must be Frankie. Hardy has told us so much about you."

"He has?"

"Oh, yes, he has. Now, I don't mean to be rude, but what in the world are you two doing here?"

Hardy, who had been playing with Luke in his arms, finally seemed to realize I needed help in order to survive the next few minutes. He set him down and grabbed my hand. I didn't miss his mom's eyes swing towards our hands and the tiny smile that appeared on her mouth.

"Mom, this is Frankie. Frankie, this is my mom, Janet. Mom, I kind of need a favour." He turned to me, "Red, can you promise to just trust me? I know that's hard for you, but please, I need to do this."

Trusting was my kryptonite. If I gave into it, I would surely get burned. But this was the new me and I had to start trusting someone at some point, and Hardy seemed like the safest point of entry. "Yes, I trust you Hardy."

His face lit up and his smile confirmed that putting all my eggs in the Hardy basket was going to work out for me. He turned back to his mom and a caught her staring intently at us. "Ok, Mom, what are you and Luke up to today?"

"Nothing much. It's nearly afternoon nap time, so we were going to wind down and watch some serious television and then drift off. Why?"

"Can I add Frankie to the mix?"

I stiffened. "Um, Hardy, I don't need-"

He once again turned to face me fully. "Babe, you do and this is my best short term solution for today." He gave my hand a squeeze and I wavered. I wasn't used to asking people for help and I guess I was about to take another huge step in my world. I sighed.

"Ok, but you need to make your mom aware of why I'm here and, I don't know, other stuff."

"Other stuff?"

"Yeah, you know, other stuff, like you and me stuff. She must think it's weird that you just dragged a woman into her home and asked her to babysit her without ever having met her. And also, um, I've never been around kids, so she might not really want me here."

His mom cleared her throat and I realized that she could probably hear everything we were saying. "I don't need to know the other stuff, Frankie. Hardy hasn't brought a girl here since, well, I'm sure you know. He hasn't smiled this much in the same amount of time and it doesn't take a genius to figure out how he feels about you. If he needs me to spend time with you, then spend time together we will. As for the kids part, we only have one monster today. I think you'll find you can do more than you ever imagined. Let me just get this little monkey down for his nap and then we can get to know each other." She swooped up Luke and left the room with him squealing over her shoulder.

"See, it's all good."

"All good? It's most certainly not all good. On our first official day as a couple, you are depositing me at your mother's house and expecting us to bond and for me to stay here for a very, long time. It is definitely not good. I don't do good girlfriend, Hardy."

"Good girlfriend? Stop. Please. I absolutely understand that this was a douche move on my part, but it's the only move I have today. I have to work the rest of the day and I can't work and save other people's lives if one of the lives I care about the most is in danger. I needed to get you someplace he didn't know about. My mom's house was the only answer I could come up with on such short notice." He moved in super close and whispered in my ear. "And for the record, you do better than good girlfriend, babe."

"Oh."

"Yeah, so, oh."
"I'm sorry Hardy. That makes perfect sense, but try to see it from my perspective. I've been trading one jailer for another for so long. My first chance at freedom happened last night, and it landed me back in protective care. With your mother!"
He laughed. "She's not that bad, come on. I bet you'll find you kind of even like her."

"I'm sure I will, it's just that, I'm not good with moms and kids. It's not in my skillset."

"You need a skillset to have a conversation with my mom? Wow, she's moved up in the world. And you're great with kids, you just haven't had the chance to see it. Luke will break you in gently." He grabbed a hold of my shoulders and gently massaged. "I've got to go. You gonna be ok?"

I huffed out a dramatic sigh, realizing this could very well be my only option for the time being. "Yes, I'll be fine. How long am I staying here for?"

"It's one o'clock now, I would expect I can come back for you around six or seven." He leaned in, gave me a deep goodbye kiss, gave his mom a shout out and was gone. Just like that. Left me high and dry with his mother. I flopped down onto the couch to wait for her return and try to mentally plan out my next move. I had to get back to my car so I could go home and pack some stuff. Hardy would probably want to be there with me when I did that, so I would have to ask him later on. I needed to get in and get out. I didn't feel safe there anymore.

I must have gotten lost in thought and not heard Janet come back into the living room. Before I knew it, she was sitting down beside me on the couch, had turned to face me and tucked her feet underneath her. It looked like sharing time was about to begin.

I couldn't help but marvel at this female version of Hardy. They looked a lot alike. Dark, kind eyes and brown hair with curls, hers streaked with luminescent gray strands. I could tell he got his saintly patience from her too as she had yet to speak. She was waiting me out, just looking at me like she was professionally trained in the art of making someone talk. She knew me already. I was the girl who couldn't stand awkward silence. George thrived in awkward silenceville, me, not so much.

"Well, ah, thanks for having me."

"Of course. I don't get to see Hardy as often as I want, so any time he comes is great. Even if it is to deposit his heretofore unknown girlfriend in my living room."

"Well, if it makes you feel any better, I didn't even know I was his girlfriend until yesterday."

She barked out a laugh. "That sounds like my boy."

"Hm, yes. He is relentless, that's for sure."

"Do you want to tell me why you're here?"

Did I? I shocked myself by hearing myself in my head scream yes! "You had better get a drink or something and sit back and get comfortable. It's a long, story. Are you sure? I don't want to frighten you?"

"Sweetheart, my son fights fires for a living. I've been scared of losing him every day since he chose that profession. I've learned to live with the fear, push it aside and live my life to its fullest potential. I can tell you have demons. Why don't you give some of them to us to take care of?"

And that's when I knew. I finally knew that I wasn't doomed to live a life of being taken for granted, a life of duty and destiny. I had found my home, so I told her my story, and together, we cried when it was over. I cried tears of release and she cried tears that were for her own reasons that I may never know.

Chapter 39

Frankie

I had fallen in love with Janet. I had no idea this is what moms could be like. My own mother cared only for her stupid reputation and bank account, not for the torture her daughter was enduring right before her very eyes. We were in the middle of a particularly embarrassing teenaged story about Hardy, when I heard his truck pull up. Luke had been picked up by his dad, and dinner had long been over. I felt so safe there and that I wanted to stay forever. I didn't know how I was ever going to convey those feelings to Janet. Hardy, I could speak to him with my heart and body, but I needed her to know, what today had meant to me.

He came through the front door and I stole a brief moment to just blatantly check him out. His hair was tousled like he had been recently running his hands through it. I noticed he did this when he was stressed or lost in deep thought. His jawline was covered with lite stubble that I knew would feel delicious against my soft skin later that night. He was dressed in his navy work uniform and if I've said it before, I'll say it again, not much beats a good looking guy in a uniform. He had that stereotype locked down. His chest was broad, his legs long and he stood comfortably with his rough hands on his hips.

"Had your fill?"

I smiled a relaxed, wide smile. "Almost."

"Frankie Cain, did you just crack a joke? Mom, what did you do to her?" He crossed the room and shoved me over towards the middle of the couch. "Where is my sullen and serious girl?"

Before I could take offense to that statement, he attacked me with those rough and ready fingers right where it counts, in my hips, where I was the most ticklish. I screeched and gathered myself up into a protective ball and tried to get his hands off me. "Hardy," I screamed totally out of breath from laughing so hard. "Stop, please."

"I'll never stop if it means I can hear you laughing like this." He tickled harder and in a wider range on my body. "Never." He inserted his best attempt at an evil laugh and I lost my composure.

A few minutes later, with the threat of losing my bladder control all over him, he finally relented and stopped attacking me. I sat up and tried to straighten myself, but it was no use. My crazy hair had come out of its' messy bun and my shirt was twisted and had somehow become tucked into my undies. I pulled it out and tried to tidy myself up while trying not to embarrass myself.

"So," Hardy began. "What did you two get up to today?"

His mom jumped in before I could. "Girl stuff. Do you need some dinner?"

"No, I ate at the station. What kind of girl stuff?"

"None of your business. Now, are you staying long or moving on? I was heading out to the movies shortly, but if you're staying, I'll cancel."

He smiled at his mom and my heart melted just a little bit more for this man. You could see in his eyes how much love and respect he had for her. He leaned over and whispered something in her ear. "You go. We're getting out of here and heading home." He turned to me, "ready?"

I had no idea what that was about, but decided to let it go. Just another thing I had missed out on. Harmless secrets between family members. Instead, I got secrets that killed and destroyed people.

He pulled me up and wrapped me in his usual protective bear hug. I wasn't used to being hugged, or even touched, so it always took me a second to reciprocate. I snuggled into his warmth, taking a moment to inhale his intoxicating scent without seeming too stalkerish. I was a smell kind of girl and he smelled of woods, and fire and man.

He grabbed my hand, leaned over and gave his mom and kiss on the cheek and pulled us to head out the door. I let go of his and hand with an impulse I didn't quite understand, went back to his mom and gave her a Hardy hug while whispering my own secret message into her ear. "Thanks for today and for Hardy."

Before I entirely lost my cool, I lost eye contact with everyone around me and raced outside to his truck, hopped in and began analyzing my momentous day.

Chapter 40

Frankie

We spent the entire night memorizing each other's bodies in front of the fire, then in bed, then in the kitchen getting a snack. I was utterly exhausted, but the ice around my heart was slowly dripping away leaving a warm, pulsing beat in its' wake.

The next week was spent in much the same pattern. Wake up, make love, get dropped off at Janet's where I spent the days helping her with Luke and learning all about Hardy and his sisters. His dad had passed away a few years ago and his mom was more than happy to fill time with me. She got lonely quickly after Luke went home each day and I found myself looking forward to our dinner time talks waiting for Hardy to show up.

My life was peaceful and exciting and I was in love. I needed to tell Hardy how I felt. I was just so damn scared. I hadn't heard from Patrick or the girls telling me he was on the move in a few days. I only had one major problem. I was completely out of clothes. I needed to make a stop at my house to pack some more clothes and possibly squeeze in a painting session or at least pack my paints and move them to Hardy's.

Which lead right into my other problem, Hardy. He wasn't letting me out of his sight, with the exception of when I went to his mothers. I didn't want him to have to take me home after a twelve hour shift, so I figure I was going to have to work on his mom. Surely Patrick wasn't going to be a problem anymore? I decided to try the as close to the truth route as my first option.

"Janet?"

"Yes?"

"What would you say to loaning me your car today?"

She looked at me with mother's eyes. Those eyes that always seemed to know everything going on inside my brain. "Where ya headed? I thought you were supposed to stick close to me?"
"Well, I have some things I need to do and Hardy keeps me behind closed doors all day, every day. I just need to grab some stuff from my house, maybe spend some time painting or hanging on the beach? I'm going a little crazy. When we leave here, we head right to Hardy's, then back here the next day. I just some space."

"What does my son think?"

"He doesn't know?" I crossed my fingers behind my back, and my toes for good measure.

She had a great poker face. I wasn't sure which way she was leaning until she scooped up her keys and threw them at me. "On one condition."

"Ok."

"You text Hardy and let him know." Crap, that wasn't going to work out. Hardy was doing his best caveman impression lately. "Once you're there." And she totally redeemed herself.

I sat down behind the wheel and immediately started to second guess myself. Was he still out there? He couldn't be. It had been days since I had last had any contact with him. The police hadn't seen him around and George and Sam hadn't heard any rumblings in our circle of friends. I took a deep breath, started the car and headed back to my rental. That's what it had become to me. Hardy's place was home, this was just my rented beach house.

I thought about Hardy all the way there. He was it for me. Once I had cleared out my stuff from the rental I was done dancing around my feelings. I was going to cook him a fantastic late dinner. We would take a walk on the beach and I would tell him all the things I was feeling about him and anything and everything else he wanted to know about me. I loved this man with all my heart and it was time I let in all the love he was offering to give and return it back to him.

I parked the car in my driveway and swiped open my cell and sent Hardy a quick text.

> Hey. Just grabbing a few things from my place. I'm out of sexy granny panties. Grabbing clothes and paints and then back to your mom's.

Red, r u for real?

> What?

I'm coming. Don't get out of the car and lock the door.

> Hardy, I'm fine, K? Please, let me do this.

Don't like it.

> I'm aware.

There was a definite break in the flow. He was stewing, I knew it.

Fine. Text me every 5 min. If I don't hear from you, I'm coming.

> K. I love you, you know right?

Baby.

> Shit, I didn't mean to tell you by text. But, I love u. I love u. I love u. See ya.

I closed the phone and plunked it down in the cup holder. I took two deep breaths in, trying not to think about what I found the last time I was in here. I burst out of the car, found my key and ran into the house. I immediately went into the bedroom and grabbed my other suitcase and began stuffing everything I could into it. It didn't take long as I hardly had much to start with.

I started breathing a little easier as so far, there was no sign of anyone else being here or having had been here. I lugged my now full suitcase to the front door when I saw a movement out of the corner of my eye. I was jumpy and now apparently, seeing things. When I looked outside, there was nothing there.

I walked back into the kitchen and looked at the clock and cursed. I had been inside more than five minutes. And I had left my phone outside in the car. "Damn," I whispered under my breath, for some reason feeling like I needed to whisper. "I had better grab my phone," I continued whispering to myself.

I turned to head back to the door, when it all went very wrong. I saw a shadow flashing quickly by, when before I could figure out what the hell it was, I felt a huge pain in my side and then nothing.

Chapter 41

Hardy

Fuck. She loved me. And she sent it in a text, from her car, where he psycho ex was stalking her. Five minutes had rolled by and she wasn't texting like we agreed to. I didn't want to come off all caveman like she accused me of, but I was starting to freak out, just a little. It was going on ten minutes since the last time she was supposed to check in. What had my mom been thinking, letting her go out?

I knew I shouldn't blame my mom, but someone was lurking out there, and I hadn't wanted to alarm Frankie, but her ex hadn't made a return trip to LA that anyone around here knew about. I also didn't want to tell Frankie I knew how high the stakes were in his end game. Senator Patrick Marks, rumoured next biggest and brightest star in the Republican's lineup.

He had a shit ton to lose and if Frankie let out even a small amount of his secrets, he was done for. My pencil tapping had reached its' peak. I was even annoying myself. I wanted to give her some space and show her I wasn't the overbearing oaf she thought I was, but I wasn't going to be able to last much longer.

As if I had summoned it, the alarm rang out and the team sprang into action. I jumped up and began to suit up, even though I rarely went out on a call anymore. I was working my way into my coveralls when I heard dispatch repeat the address and the type of emergency they could be expecting. 1091 Sea Breeze Way.

"Frankie." Fuck me. This couldn't be happening. I ran out into the garage, barking out orders to my crew. Everyone was working on getting the hell out of the station as quickly as possible, but it felt like we were all moving in slow motion. "Guys, let's move out. Fuck, get the fuck out and in this truck now."

My voice had reached panic mode and they all sensed it. Eight pairs of eyes paused to see what had their chief cursing them out. "Move it, Manson," I yelled at our newest recruit. I looked at Will and tried to mind meld the sense of urgency into his brain without saying her name. They would have an issue with me coming if they knew we were heading to Frankie's house. All of them except Will. He has been there through it all. Through this very same fucked up scenario the last time it happened to me.

I mouthed her name to him and he got it. He took over the directions and I finished getting dressed.

Ten agonizing minutes later, we were nearly there, and my sense of dread had multiplied tenfold. It was a big fire. We didn't need the dispatcher to tell us that, we could see it miles away. I was a bloody mess of emotions. This surely could not be happening to me again. It appeared that I needed to start buying lottery tickets, because, indeed, it was happening to me again. She may not have been my wife, but she was my everything. I knew I couldn't handle what was going to meet us when we got there.

A neighbour had called it in not that long ago, hopefully she had a chance to get out. In a perfect world, her car wouldn't be in the driveway and my phone would immediately start beeping from all the texts she was sending me. Ha, when had life treated me fairly.

I held on and stared out at the road running by trying to create some sense of calm in the chaos. We turned the final corner onto her short road and sure enough, my worst nightmare had come true. Her car was parked in the driveway. I leapt off even though we were still moving, and let her car break my momentum.

"Hardy!" Will was screaming for me, but I was done waiting around. I needed in there but I wasn't stupid enough to barge in unprepared. I needed to get her out alive and I needed my guys to get that done.

"Ok," I ordered. "Will and I will go in the back. Josh and Manson, you're around front at the ocean entrance. I don't have to tell you to be careful, but God, please do. My girl is in there, please, let's get her back to me."

I could see the shock on their faces as well as the doubt that I could handle what was about to potentially come our way. I didn't have to time to convince anyone I was not leaving my post. I just found her. I was not losing her.

The fire hadn't reached the rear of the house yet, so we moved in through the back door. It opened easily and we figured it must not have been locked prior to the fire. It was hot, but not a risky entrance. We burst into her home and I signalled to Will to head into the kitchen and I would search the bedroom.

I found her there, sprawled on her bed, the room in flames, completely unconscious.

"Frankie," I screamed under my mask. "Baby, wake up."

It was so fucking useless to scream. I maneuvered myself to the closest safe spot and quickly thought up my plan of action, trying desperately to step back from the scene and think this route out clinically.

Will burst into the room letting me know the rest of the house was clear of real, live people and that getting Frankie out and containing the fire were our two priorities now.

I smashed her back window and yelled for some water into the room, all the time, keeping one eye on her. It was then I noticed that we had bigger problems than just the fire. She was bleeding from her stomach. It looked like she had been shot.

"WILL! SHE'S BLEEDING OUT. HELP ME GET HER OUT OF HERE!"

I was panicking and losing my shit, but I didn't care. She needed more help than what we could give her and the closest hospital was fifteen miles away.

We were finally able to control the flames on one side of the bed and gently and strategically scoop her up and carry her out the back door, into the waiting ambulance that had pulled up shortly after we did.

I ripped off my mask and helmet and lunged up into the back of the ambulance. I turned to Will, my second in command and didn't have to say anything once again. He would take care of things. The fire was coming under control. There were no winds and it called for rain later on this evening. They would be fine. They had been here without me many times.

Frankie needed me and I couldn't abandon her. She needed me. She wasn't going to be fucking alone. I gave Will a chin lift and the doors slammed shut and we were on our way, the EMTs communicating with each other with hand signals and murmured words. I knew what this meant and It wasn't anything good.

I felt a drop of water hit my hand and realized I was falling apart. Tears were escaping and blurring my vision and I felt so out of control, that I let them fall.

The radio buzzed and crackled and alerted the emerg team of our estimated arrival time and Frankie's status. They whispered it into the unit, but I knew what that meant too and it only made the tears worse.

"Frankie, you fucking leave me today and I will personally smack your sorry, sweet ass. You are not leaving me, baby. Not today, not ever."

I saw the female attendant wipe a tear from her eye and knew she got me. They bent their heads down and got to work trying to save my girlfriend's life.

Chapter 42

Frankie

I had a mean case of déjà vu. Beeping noises, irritating fluorescent lighting, hushed voices and eyes that felt glued together and in no way would be opening soon.

Too bad my damn brain didn't agree with my eyes. It felt the need to assess the situation. I felt like a fog had descended on my brain. I couldn't find my way out and slowly willed myself to retreat back to wherever it was I came from.

Before I left to go back to that amazing, peaceful place, I felt a presence give me a little tug. A gentle push forward instead of back. I began to notice other things right around that time. Someone was touching my hand. Warm and rough fingers had a death grip on me. I could hear a low, male voice, mixed with a mix of different female voices.

I could smell sharp, clean scents and underneath me, a hard, plastic bed. It hit me then with a force I couldn't ignore. Moving forward was my only option and all signs pointed to me being in the hospital. Oh no, no, no, no. Not again. He had put me here again.

With a gasp, I catapulted into whatever situation met me in this stark, bright room. I wasn't prepared for the reality, but none the less, it appeared to be time.

I pried my eyes open, feeling like my eyelashes were separating from my eyes while doing so, and took in my surroundings before anyone in the room could realize I was awake. Yup, I was in the hospital, and it appeared I was in some sort of ICU unit based on the amount of machines and the lack of privacy I had.

The female voices I heard were Sam and a nurse, and the warm, hand I felt belonged to a dark mop of brown hair that was attached to Hardy. I struggled to remember how I had gotten here. Before they noticed I was awake, I tried to assess my injuries. My chest hurt like hell, my head was in the same boat, but otherwise, I didn't feel like I had any broken body parts. I generally felt like shit, but if I was in the ICU, that was to be expected.

My heart rate must have been gradually changing on the monitor, because the nurse suddenly whipped around while talking to Sam to inspect it. She looked at me and smiled. "Welcome back, Frances. You had us worried there for a bit."

She moved out of the way for a minute and I got a clear vision of Sam, bawling and Hardy, pretty much doing the same.

"I'm going to page the doctor. You two have a couple of minutes before he comes, but once he gets here, we'll need her for a good hour." She left to go find my doctor and I didn't know what to say to make these two stop crying. The two strongest people I knew, weeping in front of me wasn't something I knew how to handle.

"Please," I croaked. "You guys are freaking me out."

Sam blew her nose and swiped at her now running mascara. "Shut the fuck up, Franks. I cannot believe this is the second time I've been called to your nearly dead bedside in the past twelve months. It's so not ok with me. I was in Ireland for God sakes. With a man! Do you understand how I freaked out I was? You have got to stop taking these matters into your own hands." She leapt on top of me, causing me to squeak out in agony, enveloped me in a giant bear hug and planted a big one on my cheek.

"Ok, I love you, but I've got to get back to the airport to catch a flight back to set. You're awake and in good hands. I want you on a plane visiting me in the next month if possible. No excuses other than a doctor's note. Got that Hardy?"

She spun around, pointed a perfectly manicured nail at Hardy and flounced out of the room.

"Hey."

I slowly turned my aching head towards him. "Hey."

It turned out, I did remember why I was in there. It seems I had some apologizing to do. Once again, I just ran headfirst into a dangerous situation, thinking I could handle it alone, not thinking of the others that could get hurt by my thoughtlessness.

"I'm sorry." I hardly recognized my voice. It was painful to talk, but I needed to get some things out.

"Frankie, stop talking."

"But you told me–"

"I know what I told you. But it's over now. Now, we only have what happens next. He's in jail. Your nightmare is over. You are free to go where you want, when you want. You don't have to worry about him anymore. You will have to testify against him and that's going to be hard, but you will get through it." His eyes were red. His stubble grown in. He must have been here around the clock.

"Hardy–"

"No, Frankie. You don't need to talk. I know this is where we end and you begin. You're free, babe. You can go back to your life. You don't need to stick around here anymore and I'm trying hard to be good with that. I know you need your freedom. I just have to get used to accepting that. Of course, you'll have to come back for the hearing, but otherwise, it's over."

I took a deep breath. He so was not doing this to me. Not happening Mr. Hanson. "Hardy," my voice cracked and I swallowed thinking it must have been days since I had drank any water. "Listen to me now. I'm sorry I didn't think about you and your mom and your team before I went flying into my home thinking I could beat him. I'm sorry it nearly got me killed and probably got a lot of people in a lot of trouble. But, I'm not sorry at the same time. He's gone. I'm alive and yes, I am free. Free to choose things, stuff, life."

"I love you Hardy. I love you so much it makes me nauseous thinking I might have left this earth without making sure you knew how badly I loved you. You're not deciding for me where I go from here. I'm going wherever you're going and since I know you love this place like no other place, that's where I'm staying. And I'm staying with you. For as long as you'll have me. And I'm claiming your mom as my own until she tells me it's uncomfortable for everyone the way I call her mom in public."

I raised a hand littered with tubes and needles as best I could to rub against his prickly face. "Can I stay?"

And the man tears that broke my heart all over again flowed freely from his eyes and he nodded his head and leaned in for a kiss which I was so not on board for. Unknown amount of days without dental hygiene wasn't a good way to start off a new life together. "My breath, Hardy."

"Is awful, but I don't give a shit. You're staying and we'll both get some morning breath experience when you move in with me and wake up beside me every single day."

"Move in with you, like, for real?"

"No more pretending. It's me and you. I'm sure but you need to be sure, so take your time and when you're ready, I'm here waiting. I love you baby." He leaned in and gave me another tiny kiss on the corner of my mouth. "I was so scared," he whispered against my mouth. "I didn't know how I was going to survive without you." Another soft kiss. "Baby." He raised his head and I swore I would never hurt this loving, amazing man ever again.

The curtain swung open and a gaggle of doctor's surged in, not realizing, or caring they had interrupted my life changing moment with Hardy.

Epilogue

Hardy

My heart rate is skyrocketing and I'm pretty sure passing out is not an option. She wouldn't kill me, but more likely, she would spend the rest of our lives reminding me of what a wuss I was. I take a deep breath in and let it out and shift slightly to relieve the pain in my back from being bent over in this awkward position.

"Come on baby, you can do this. You so got this."

"Fuck off Hardy."

I heard a snicker behind me and knew Sam had finally arrived. Thank God. I had been through this before, but it never gets easy.

"Sam, thank God. Please come and hold her other hand."

Sam walked over to the bed where my gorgeous wife lay, about to give birth to our first child. She wanted to do this at home, in our bed and it took a lot of convincing from her and our midwife before I relented. Our room looked like a war zone, littered with giant exercise balls, wet towels, the midwife's supplies and the usual mess the room had in it.

Propped up, on the edge of our king sized bed, was my little Red. I was behind her, with my legs around her body and let her use my chest as a safe place to rest and push against. Sam had dropped her bags and come around to the beach side of the bed. She pulled up the waiting chair and took a hold of Frankie's right hand. Thank God for that. I lost full functionality of my right hand about an hour ago.

"Sam," Frankie huffed out. "You made it."

"You doubted me? That hurts Franks. Hurts right here." She made a dramatic gesture with her free hand over her heart. It was then, I heard a soft chuckle coming from the door frame.

I looked up and saw a man leaning against the frame, smiling, with eyes only for Sam. I looked at him, then pointedly looked at Sam. Why in the hell had she brought a perfect stranger into our house to witness my wife's lady bits and the delivery of our child? He looked kind of scary, what with the tallness, the full beard and the tattoos.

"Hardy, Frankie, meet Brennan. Brennan, Frankie and Hardy."

Frankie squealed, and I wasn't sure if it was because we were nearly ready to push or for some other reason. "Sam," she whispered. "He came."

"Yes, Franks. He sure did." Something big was happening here, and I was really feeling out of the loop. Sam was making mooney eyes at this Brennan guy and he looked back at her as if she was the be all and end all to him. Kind of how I looked at Frankie every day. But he had something else behind his eyes. Pain, anger and something I couldn't put my finger on.

"Ah, you're welcome to stay, since it looks like the girls want you to, but could you please keep your eyes north of my wife?"

He laughed and just turned and walked out of the room. I could hear him talking to Chuck who was freaking out in the hallway, having been banned from the bedroom. "What the hell, Sam?"

"Hardy," Frankie said. "It's ok. Relax. Sam needs him right now, and I need Sam, so we get Brennan." She ended that statement with an ear piercing scream and I instantly forgot about the stranger now roaming our house.

The midwife looked up. "Ok, it's time to push. Ready, Frankie?"

She nodded and we all got into position, excited and scared at the impending arrival. As she pushed and did all the hard work required, my mind drifted to the last time I had been witness to the birth of my child. I knew I was going to lose my manhood once again and bawl like a baby, but I couldn't help but feel such huge amounts of joy. This was our second chance to be parents again. We weren't going to take this job lightly and we knew all too well, the heartache of losing a child. I sent my daily thanks to the universe for blessing me with two amazing wives, who gifted me with my children and got back to focusing in on the activities happening in front of me.

With one final push, our son was delivered into the world, screaming bloody murder and looking for his mom and dad. The midwife laid him on Frankie's chest and through our tears of joy, we welcomed Will Cain Hanson into our life and created a family that would love each other, support each other and lift each other up.

I bent over the two most important people in my life and whispered, "I love you Frances Hanson. Love you little man."

Watch the story of Sam and Brennan unfold in Book 3 of the Sisters Series, World Apart.

Coming January 2016.

Sign up to receive exclusive content and exciting news:
www.hollymortimer.com

Follow me on Facebook :
https://www.facebook.com/hollymortimerromancewriter

Tweet me! : @mortimerwrites

Check out my inspiration boards on Pinterest:
https://www.pinterest.com/hmortimer/

Made in the USA
Charleston, SC
12 September 2015